"It doesn't have to be a real marriage."

Chase was determined to have his way on this whether she liked it or not. "At least not in the conventional sense."

"Well, that's a relief." Merri looked at him, a mix of exasperation and cynicism in her glacier-green eyes.

He regarded her seriously, aware he had a respon̶s̶i̶b̶i̶l̶i̶t̶y̶ ̶h̶e̶r̶e̶. "Its only purpose will be to help us mee̶͟_____

Merri _____ r to your childr̶_____

Chase _____ s and clasped her delicate hands around her knee. When had she gotten so all-out beautiful? "While keeping you as the mother they know and love."

"People will talk."

"You're worried our relationship wouldn't stay platonic."

Merri stared at him, knowing a guy as healthy and virile and sexy as Chase had to have needs, too. She kept her eyes locked with his, even as her heart raced like a wild thing in her chest. "Aren't you?"

Dear Reader,

There's never a good time for a crisis, particularly during the Thanksgiving and Christmas holidays. But the "season of giving" has a way of bringing family and friends together—when we're lucky, in ways that last forever.

Chase Armstrong has been avoiding the heartache at home for years, but finally decides to return to his Texas roots. He knows it will be tough seeing the only family he has left. He doesn't expect to be hit with news that will change his life.

Merri Duncan is worried about Chase's homecoming, too. She's been wondering about his plans regarding the niece and nephew he has long neglected. And she knows he isn't likely to approve of what she has done to the Armstrong clan's Broken Arrow ranch in his absence.

What neither Merri nor Chase expects is the stark realization that turns their lives upside down. Experience has taught her that wanting something to happen doesn't make it so. But both are willing to do the honorable thing and bring the family together the way it should be, even if it means big sacrifices for both of them. Because in big, bold, brash Laramie County, family always comes first.

Happy reading,

Cathy Gillen Thacker

The Texas Rancher's Marriage

CATHY GILLEN THACKER

HARLEQUIN®
entertain, enrich, inspire™

Recycling programs
for this product may
not exist in your area.

ISBN-13: 978-0-373-75432-8

THE TEXAS RANCHER'S MARRIAGE

Copyright © 2012 by Cathy Gillen Thacker

ABOUT THE AUTHOR

Cathy Gillen Thacker is married and a mother of three. She and her husband spent eighteen years in Texas and now reside in North Carolina. Her mysteries, romantic comedies and heartwarming family stories have made numerous appearances on bestseller lists, but her best reward, she says, is knowing one of her books made someone's day a little brighter. A popular Harlequin Books author for many years, she loves telling passionate stories with happy endings, and thinks nothing beats a good romance and a hot cup of tea! You can visit Cathy's website at www.cathygillenthacker.com for more information on her upcoming and previously published books, recipes and a list of her favorite things.

Books by Cathy Gillen Thacker

HARLEQUIN AMERICAN ROMANCE

Chapter One

"Breathe."

Merri Duncan turned to her best friend, Emily McCabe Reeves, aware she had never been so nervous in her life.

"That obvious, hmm?" Merri drawled, glad she had thought to get a babysitter for the twins. Right now, as they all waited for their beloved guest of honor to show, she could barely contain herself, never mind two rowdy preschoolers.

Over two hundred other local residents and family friends had gathered on the Armstrong ranch. Texas barbecue scented the air. A country and western band warmed up next to the dance floors set up on the lawn.

"I know the last time Chase was home was pretty awful," Emily commiserated.

"An understatement," Merri murmured back. Together, she and Chase had weathered the aftermath of a horrific helicopter crash, and buried her sister and his brother. Then Merri had taken custody of Sasha and Scott's eight-week-old infants, and Chase had headed back to the army field hospital in the Middle East.

Four and a half years had passed.

Chase hadn't been back to the States since.

Although Merri and the twins had heard from him sporadically—mostly at Christmas, and on birthdays—the big,

8 *The Texas Rancher's Marriage*

strapping Texan never disclosed what he intended to do, long-term.

If anything... All Merri knew for sure was that he had finally completed his tour of duty and had accepted a job at the Laramie Community Hospital.

She and the twins were now settled comfortably on the once-luxurious ranch where Chase and his brother had grown up, and where her business, though still small, was thriving. In addition to the excitement and upheaval of Chase's homecoming, the Christmas holidays were approaching and Thanksgiving was just a few days away.

Merri released a tremulous sigh. Life sure had a way of taking unexpected turns.

And she had the nagging feeling that as soon as she and Chase talked about the information she had accidentally discovered, her already complicated life would take another unscripted detour. Merri knew from firsthand experience that the circumstances of the twins' origins would not be dealt with as simply as she had initially hoped. And soon, like it or not, Chase would realize that, too.

Misreading the reason behind Merri's obvious apprehension, Emily gave her friend an encouraging hug. "Stop worrying! It's going to be a great welcome home party for Chase."

Merri sure hoped so. The returning trauma surgeon deserved to be celebrated for the true hero he was.

And she...she needed to stop agonizing.

Chase was a decent guy, and he would do the right thing, just as he always had. In fact, that was likely the reason he was back—to lend a hand in the way only he could.

Although what he would want to tell people about the truth of their situation was as much a mystery as it ever had been.

Emily smiled and lifted her arm in an excited wave as

her husband's pickup truck turned into the long, tree-lined drive. "Here they come now!"

Merri slipped into the ranch house and emerged with the twins in hand.

Curly blond heads tilted upward and their big brown eyes gleamed excitedly as they watched the truck come to a halt. A tall man emerged from the passenger seat, and when Merri got a look at Chase Armstrong, her heart took a little leap.

She hadn't realized until this very moment how scared she had been. That something would happen over there and the sexy physician wouldn't come back. At least not alive.

But there was no question the ruggedly handsome, sandy-haired man was very *much* alive.

His skin was tanned, his shoulders every bit as wide and inviting as she recalled, his body lean and hard and solidly muscled enough to make her insides quiver. He should have looked tired and unkempt after the long flight, but his face was cleanly shaved, his short, clipped hair as neat and clean as the army fatigues he wore.

Dark sunglasses shaded his beautiful amber eyes, and a slow grin tugged at the corners of his sensual lips as, with an unhurried stride, he moved toward the crowd waiting to greet him.

A cheer went up.

Caught in the raw emotion of the moment, Merri found herself cheering, too.

The crowd parted. Chase continued on his mission, coming closer still. Then he was standing directly before her and the kids, lazily taking off his sunglasses and slipping them into the pocket of his shirt.

At six foot four, he had always dwarfed her five-foot-seven frame. Today was no exception; she had to tilt her head back to look up at him.

And as their eyes met and held, there was absolutely no clue in his about what he intended to do about this fix they were in. Or when he planned to talk to her about the biggest conundrum of all.

CHASE KNEW COMING BACK TO the only real home he had ever known was going to be difficult.

Just being on the ranch reminded him of the family he'd lost and the nonstop disappointment life had brought his way.

Seeing the crowd gathered on the property he could no longer call home made it even harder.

It reminded him of the aftermath of the dual funerals, when everyone who had ever cared about Scott and Sasha had stopped by to pay their respects. And the burials of his parents, in the half-dozen years before that.

There had been a lot of loss on the Broken Arrow Ranch. Now the future of it was embodied in the two impossibly cute preschoolers holding on to Merri Duncan's hands.

Their sweet, cherubic appearance was no surprise. He had seen dozens of photos and the occasional video of the kids during the years he had been overseas, so was well-versed in the milestone events of Jeffrey and Jessalyn's infant and toddler days.

But Merri had always managed to keep herself out of the photos.

And now Chase could not help but be stunned by the changes he saw. Her shoulder-length, golden-blond hair was still thick and silky, her face just as elegantly beautiful, her wide, friendly smile as arresting as ever. But there was a soft, maternal air about her now. A tenderness in the way she gently clasped the twins' hands, and held them even closer to her sides. A new maturity—as well as a lingering question—in her pretty, glacier-green eyes. And a lithe, sexy body that made him all too aware just how long it had been since he'd been physically close to any woman.

Too long.

Their eyes locked and his heartbeat kicked up.

Warning himself to play it cool, he leaned over to give her a casual one-armed hug and a light kiss on the brow.

"Welcome home," she said in a husky voice.

Her emotion was contagious. Chase cleared his throat to get rid of the catch in his own voice. "Thanks." He released Merri as quickly and efficiently as he had hugged her, and then knelt before the kids.

Jeffrey and Jessalyn regarded him shyly.

"Say hello to Chase," Merri prodded.

An awkward silence fell. The twins stared at him mutely, probably still deciding if he was friend or foe. To his disappointment, they seemed inclined to put him in the latter category.

Deciding it would be best not to push them, Chase looked into their eyes. He smiled at them reassuringly once again, letting them know they could trust him, then stood. "It's okay," he told a concerned Merri under his breath. "We'll have a chance to get acquainted later."

Eyes glistening, she nodded, as if suddenly not trusting herself to speak.

Chase knew exactly how she felt. Confronted with the only real family he had left, he had a lump in his throat, too.

He had never expected to feel so alone and adrift at this point in his life. But maybe that would change now that he was back in Laramie. Back where he'd grown up, Chase thought, as familiar figures came forward to shake his hand and give him a hug.

"Hey, Chase!" His old high school classmate, Travis Anderson, stepped up to shake his hand. "Didn't think we'd ever see you again!"

"Great to have you back in Texas!" His former high school English teacher beamed. "Don't leave us again, you understand? We missed you!"

"I was beginning to think you'd left us for good," the owner of Sonny's Barbecue teased, giving him a slap on the back...and a hug. "Come by and see me when you get a little time."

And so it went. Everyone complaining good-naturedly about how long he'd been gone, worrying he'd up and leave Laramie County again, warning him that if he did take off again their hearts would be broken beyond repair. The twins' eyes got even wider as they soaked it all in.

"I think you'd all survive," Chase joshed back when the rush of sentiment got a little much. Any more of this and they'd have him getting all weepy, too.

He looked around for help. Merri seemed to have faded into the background, but members of the band—also old pals of his—got the hint. They immediately started playing a rowdy rendition of the perennial Texas party favorite, "Friends in Low Places."

An appreciative roar went up. Everyone joined in the raucous singing and swaying. Dancing soon followed. And, to Chase's joy, the real homecoming began.

HOURS LATER, CHASE AND MERRI stood side by side as the last of the taillights disappeared down the drive. It was the first time they'd been alone since he arrived, and Chase was more than a little aware of her. Not that this was a surprise. The first time he had seen her, at his brother's engagement party, he'd wanted her. But Merri had been living with another guy and practically engaged, so he'd done the honorable thing and walked away.

She turned to him now with heartfelt apology. "I'm sorry about the cool reception you received from the twins."

Cognizant that he probably should have expected as much, given how little contact they'd had, Chase shrugged. "Don't worry about it."

"I tried to prepare them for actually meeting you, instead of just seeing your face on the screen in a video chat, or hearing your voice on the phone."

Which, Chase reflected, given some of the rough-and-tumble sites where he had been stationed, hadn't happened all that frequently. He tore his eyes from the curves beneath Merri's snug-fitting T-shirt, cropped denim jacket and jeans. Her burgundy western boots were nice, too. Obviously custom, from Monroe's. He recognized the signature Texas rose hidden in the fancy feminine embroidery adorning the sides.

"But I'm not sure they believed it was really going to happen," Merri continued, oblivious of the impact she was having on him. "Or understood what your coming here would mean to them." She released a sigh. "Because at the time I told them, I wasn't sure if you were just coming for a visit or staying long-term."

Had she always smelled this good? Like lavender…and woman? Wishing he could make a move on her, without complicating things unnecessarily, Chase shrugged. "I'm sorry about that." Because the kids were already inside, fast asleep, he remained on the porch, speaking quietly with Merri. His gaze roved her upturned face. Although she'd been gorgeous in daylight, she looked even more radiant in the soft glow of the porch light.

Gruffly, he confessed, "I didn't know what I was going to do myself till a few days ago." It had been a tough decision to make. Complicated by the fact that if he came back to stay, Merri was going to expect him to be an uncle to the kids, and behave in a brotherly fashion to her. And his feelings for her were anything but fraternal. Although, thankfully for both of them, she didn't know that.

Merri studied him, a new realism shining in her lovely green eyes. As if the fairy-tale wishes she had once harbored had faded, and she knew now what life was—and what it wasn't. She stepped a little closer, further inundating him in her deliciously feminine scent. "You were really thinking of reenlisting?"

Chase ignored the mounting desire generated by her closeness; and the sight of her running a delicate hand through the soft, thick layers of her honey-blond hair. "It's important work. I made a lot of good friends over there. But…there's important work to be done here, too, and I also have a lot of friends here, so…I finally decided to come home."

Chase saw her shiver a little in the cooling night air. She pulled the edges of her jacket together, but not before he noted her physical reaction to the declining temperature.

"I'm glad you did." Flushing self-consciously, she said, "I know the kids are, too. They just don't know how to express it yet. In any case, I prepared the guest room for you."

"You don't have to put me up tonight," Chase said. "I can sleep in an on-call room at the hospital, till I have time to find a place." Thanks to the local auto dealer's cooperation in making an advance sale, he even had a brand-new pickup truck to drive, waiting in the parking area next to the ranch house.

A mixture of disappointment and guilt colored her expression. "This is your home."

"It was once," Chase agreed, his tone flat, as old decisions neither of them had anything to do with came back to haunt them once again. He brushed aside the hurt he'd felt for years now. The hurt that had helped keep him away, and made him wonder if he should return to Laramie County at all. "But not anymore."

MERRI WONDERED IF THIS was the reason behind the rift that had existed between Chase and his younger brother. One that had seemed to only get bigger as time passed, reaching a point of no return shortly before Chase went off to war. Which, of course, made his eventual generosity regarding the birth of the twins even more difficult for her to understand.

Now that he was back, however, and going to be part of the twins' lives, it was time she rectified that.

"I never understood why your mother willed the entire property to Scott." The one-sided terms of the late Lydia Armstrong's estate had shocked everyone when the will had been read. Especially Chase, Merri remembered, because he hadn't known the disinheritance was coming.

He glanced up at the half-moon overhead, then restlessly walked the length of the porch that lined the large stone-and-cedar ranch house. His gaze traveled over the manicured lawn and the lush shrubbery, to the now-empty pastures. He didn't seem to find fault with anything he saw in the pastoral scene. Which was no surprise to Merri. She had done a good job as conservator of the property, on behalf of the twins, who had inherited it all upon their father's death.

Chase ignored the chain-hung swing at the end of the porch and ambled back to her side. "She figured I was a doctor. I'd make plenty of money and never have time to ranch. Whereas Scott needed a job and a place to live."

Merri knew enough about Scott and Sasha's selfishness now to realize undue pressure had been applied to the elder, ailing Armstrong, her emotions likely played upon. Because, hard as it was to admit, at the end of the day, all Merri's sister and Chase's brother had ever thought about was themselves. Their desires. Their needs.

And Chase knew it, too.

Aware it was a little too intimate to be standing there together in the semidarkness, Merri pivoted and led him inside. "Your mom could have left you half the land anyway," she said over her shoulder. "I mean, we're talking about over five thousand acres! Or Scott and Sasha could have willed the property back to you, instead of putting it in trust for their children." *And naming me as executor and guardian of that trust.*

In the living room, Chase watched her remove the screen on the fireplace. He seemed as oblivious to the chill in the air as she was sensitive to it.

"It's okay. I got over what happened a long time ago."

Had he? Truth was, Merri couldn't see how. She knelt before the hearth, and admitted with total frankness, "I still feel funny about us living here and you not. It doesn't seem right."

Chase continued to watch as she arranged the firewood. "Life's not fair. We all know that."

He was right. Merri wadded up some newspaper and stuffed it in the gaps between the oak logs. If it had been, her sister would have had functioning ovaries. She would not have required donated eggs—from Merri—to become pregnant. Had life been fair, Scott wouldn't have needed to go to Chase for his assistance, too.

Still surprised that Chase had helped Sasha and Scott out in the end, even after initially turning the couple down, Merri decided it was past time to ask the question that had been burning in her gut for several years now. Nervously, she blurted out, "What about the twins?"

Chase gave her a mystified look. "What about them?" he asked carefully.

She struck a match and lit the fire. "What are your intentions there?" she prodded.

Chase watched the paper take the flame, before turning

his gaze to Merri again. "You're their biological mother. You should be telling me how you want this to work."

Her anxiety rose. Chase was decisive in all other areas of his life. His apathy and indifference here were daunting, to say the least. "But like it or not, you're involved, too," she persisted, trying to squeeze some emotion out of him, to get him to tell her where this predicament was likely headed. "Biologically speaking, anyway."

A tense silence fell. Chase stared at her as if she had either lost her mind or was a disaster waiting to happen. "What are you talking about?" He slowly enunciated every word.

Weary of maintaining the public ruse her late brother-in-law and sister had insisted upon, Merri looked Chase square in the eye and admitted, "A few months after Scott and Sasha died, I found the paperwork from the fertility clinic, indicating that Scott received help there, too."

Chase shrugged. "Although it wasn't common knowledge, you and I both know my brother had problems in that regard, too. That he was, for all intents and purposes, as sterile as Sasha."

"Which was why you jumped in to help, just as I did."

"And," Chase continued matter-of-factly, "set him up with the top infertility specialists at the medical school I attended."

His involvement hadn't ended there and Merri knew it. Frustration mounting, she rose and walked toward him. "Look, I don't know what kind of deal you and your brother made…probably something similar to the one I made with Sasha and him. But you don't have to hide anything from me, Chase. Not anymore. I know that you 'helped out' a heck of a lot more than just setting them up with the right professionals."

Chase studied her. "I don't know what Scott told you—or

Sasha, for that matter. My brother had a way of bending the truth to suit his needs, never more so than when his back was against a wall. But I did not do what you did, Merri. I didn't offer up my genetic material to help them out." He exhaled sharply. "They asked me—before I went overseas… as you well know—but I told them I couldn't handle having a child raised by someone else, not even my own kin. It's not in me to be a spectator in my own child's life."

Merri knotted her hands in frustration. She remembered the chaos his refusal had caused among the four of them. The rift that had left Chase and his brother barely speaking. "Then why did you sign those papers, allowing Scott to use sperm you had already donated to the university for medical research, for Sasha's in vitro fertilization procedure?"

Chase's mouth dropped open in dismay. "I never signed anything."

"But you did!" Merri went to the desk, unlocked the drawer and pulled out a slender file of papers. She handed it over.

Chase studied the medical forms and legal documents. A muscle worked convulsively in his jaw. "Scott must have forged this. Damn him!"

Merri's heart sank as shock turned to comprehension. *Oh, my heaven.* "You mean…?" she croaked.

"I never gave my permission." Chase rifled through the papers, scanning them again and again, as if unable to believe what he was seeing. With anger flashing in his amber eyes, he let out a string of swear words that would have burned the ears off a nun.

Merri placed a hand over her heart, trembling, she was so upset. "So all this time… You never had a clue that you were the real father of the twins or were in any way biologically connected with them?" That certainly explained his lack of input or involvement. He hadn't thought Jessalyn and Jeffrey were family at all!

Chase sat down, scrubbed a hand over his face and dropped his head in his hands. "None whatsoever," he said miserably.

A silence fraught with heartache fell.

"So what now?" Merri asked eventually, afraid she already knew.

Chase lifted his head, already taking charge, like the kick-butt Texan he was. "We do everything and anything we have to do to make things right."

MAKING THINGS RIGHT, according to Chase's world, meant verifying facts. So as soon as the hospital lab opened the next morning, Merri and Chase and the twins were there.

Unfortunately, no sooner had they all submitted to a simple and painless DNA test than Chase was summoned to the E.R., to help out with an incoming trauma.

Subsequent surgeries had him staying in the hospital on-call room overnight. And by the time Merri and Chase got to attorney Liz Cartwright Anderson's office the following afternoon, they already had the results they had expected.

Quickly, the two of them brought Liz up to speed on everything that had happened thus far. Chase concluded with, "—I never would have given my brother permission to use my sperm."

"But you were okay with the egg donation from the beginning?" Liz asked Merri.

She nodded, still at peace with what she'd done. "I knew how important it was to my sister to have a baby. Her eggs weren't viable. So for her, to have a baby with the Duncan family genetics, harvesting my eggs and implanting them in her was the only way."

"It was still a lot to ask," Chase said fiercely.

"I understood where she was coming from." Merri turned to him. "Sasha and I never knew our father. We had lost our mother. I wanted my sister to have the baby she had always dreamed about."

And, Merri added silently, *at the time I was still living with Pierce, and thought marriage and a family for me were just around the corner, too. I thought that Sasha and I would be rearing our children together.*

"My sister had promised me I would be an integral part of the twins' lives. And for those first two months, I was there so much, helping out, I practically was a second mother." Which had made taking over, in the wake of their parents' sudden, unexpected death, a lot easier than it would have been otherwise.

"What about the secrecy?" Liz continued to make notes on the legal pad in front of her. "Were you okay with that?"

"I knew the whole thing might seem weird to some people—" Merri shot a telling look at Chase "—who would probably fixate on the fact that it was my eggs and my brother-in-law's sperm making the babies."

"Except it wasn't Scott's genetic material," Chase interrupted brusquely, all domineering Texas male. "It was mine."

Merri wished he wasn't so big, strong, sexy and by the book! "Yes, well..." Merri eyed him testily, aware his take-charge attitude was really beginning to get under her skin. Almost as much as the thought that they'd unknowingly made two babies together. "I didn't realize that at the time." So it wasn't as if she'd done something dishonorable!

"And now that you are aware?" Liz interjected, with her usual lawyerly calm.

Merri sighed, pushing away the emotion welling inside her. "It actually makes it less—" she paused, searching for the right word, as she once again met Chase's angst-filled gaze "—*controversial* to think the babies are Chase's." She gulped at the heat of awareness flaring up inside her, then turned back to Liz. "Because Chase was never married to my sister."

Chase and Liz acknowledged her sentiment with slight nods.

"But back to my willingness to stay silent..." Merri forced herself to go on. "I agreed with Sasha and Scott that it really wasn't anyone else's business how the twins were conceived. Nor would it ever have been, if they had lived to raise the twins."

But sadly, that hadn't happened.

Merri shrugged, forcing herself to continue her recollection of the heart-wrenching events that followed. "And then when Scott and Sasha died, I was named guardian of the children, as well as guardian of their estate, so..."

Nodding, Liz jumped to the logical conclusion. "You saw no reason to set the record straight."

Merri lifted her hands. "We were grieving. It didn't seem like the right time to disclose all that, in court, since I was already technically their mother...because of the guardianship. And then, a few months later, when I finally went through their things and found the paperwork identifying Chase as the biological father, I erroneously assumed that he wanted that to be kept private, too—"

Merri stopped abruptly, reeling from the memories of that tumultuous time. Of how things might have been different if she and Chase had known about his involvement. That he, too, was a parent to the children—at least biologically.

Merri swallowed hard. Aware Chase and Liz were both waiting for her to continue, she stammered. "So there was just no way I could c-come forward without making things more difficult than they already were."

"So rather than stir up a hornet's nest, you just let things be," Liz said.

"Yes. Because I thought Chase didn't want to be involved. That he didn't want to discuss it. Otherwise…I was sure he would have laid claim to the children at the time of Scott and Sasha's death."

"So you went on. Alone," Liz surmised.

"Yes," Merri admitted in a choked voice. Though she had always known, in the deepest recesses of her heart, that a day of reckoning might come.

As it finally had…

Liz looked at Chase. "What would you like to do here?"

"These kids are mine. I want to be their dad and help Merri raise them. But I also want to do everything we can to protect the twins from scandal."

"Meaning, keep this quiet," Liz asserted.

The two nodded in unison, and then Merri added, "I'm no more comfortable with the lies that started all this than Chase is. But we agree—the twins are far too young to understand."

"If they don't ever have to know, we'd rather they didn't," he added.

"So," Merri said, "if there was a way this could be handled privately…the court records sealed to ensure word never gets out…"

Liz tapped her fingers on her desk. Looked from Chase to Merri and back again. "I understand what you're asking me to do. Unfortunately, there are a couple of pretty big problems with all this," she said. "The twins turned four…"

"Last March," Merri qualified.

"Hence, in Texas, you can no longer challenge paternity based on DNA. That option ends when a child turns four, no matter what the circumstances. You can *terminate* the parental rights of Scott and Sasha, and *adopt* the children, but a judge would first have to determine if that is in their best interest. And I'll be honest." Liz sighed. "I don't see that happening. At least not in the immediate time frame you want."

Chase lifted a hand. "Wait a minute. Why would we have to adopt them when the DNA tests prove they are ours, biologically?"

"Because in Texas, in the eyes of the law, they are *not* your children," Liz explained calmly. "You terminated those legal rights when you donated the sperm and the eggs."

"Except Scott lied." Chase grimaced. "He forged my signature. I never agreed to give him that sperm to make a baby."

Liz gestured matter-of-factly. "But you *did* give sperm to the research facility. And that permission trumps any legal rights you had prior to that."

"What happened was still fraudulent," Chase insisted.

Liz nodded in solemn agreement. "You could sue. There would be a lot of ugly publicity. It would take years. Which is not what you want."

No, Merri thought miserably, it wasn't. The kids had been through enough already, being orphaned as babies and spending the past four-plus years without a father figure or steady male influence.

"Then what would be the best course?" Chase countered, obviously still determined to be a part of the twins' lives.

The attorney leaned back in her chair. "I suggest you look at the matter the way the family court will. The twins have a guardian, and they are doing well. The court is going to want to continue the status quo. So if you want to have access to the children, your best bet is to petition to be a co-guardian with Merri."

How often would Chase be around, anyway? she wondered. Given the fact that he was a surgeon, he'd probably be at the hospital all the time. When he wasn't, well, they would figure out how to coparent. It might even be good for the kids to have a man around all the time. Something she and Sasha had never had when they were young. It would give the twins a male role model, fill the void.

"I could handle that," Merri murmured.

Chase nodded in relief. "Me, too."

Liz continued to frown. "That's a very generous attitude," she acknowledged. "Unfortunately, for both of you, it's not quite that simple."

Chase and Merri groaned in unison as they waited for the ax to fall.

"You see...I know Judge Roy," Liz continued bluntly. "She is not going to grant this, even on a temporary basis, unless you are married."

Well, *that* was out of the question, Merri thought. When she married, it would be for love. Period. To her relief, Chase appeared to feel the same way.

"Isn't there another judge?" he asked Liz.

The attorney rocked back in her chair. "No. Priscilla Roy is it for Laramie County, in family court."

"Well, we can still ask," Chase insisted, as determined as ever to do the right thing. "Explain the situation to her. All Judge Roy can do is say no."

"That's true." Liz pressed her fingertips together in front of her. "But if you lose, you would then have to go to appeal, which would halt the whole process for at least a year."

Silence fell as they all thought about that.

The last thing Merri wanted was more time in limbo.

Liz leaned forward and concluded kindly, "What I suggest you do is go home, think about all this, spend some time with the kids...and figure out if there isn't some way the two of you can handle this unofficially, at least for now. Because once you start this process," she warned, "believe me, there will be no turning back."

Chapter Two

Chase settled next to Merri on the porch swing. It was a beautiful fall day, sunny and clear, with the temperature hovering around sixty degrees. Broken Arrow land stretched out as far as the eye could see. But as good as it felt to be home again—and the ranch *was* home to him, and always would be—Chase was focused on the beautiful woman seated beside him. In tailored brown slacks, ivory sweater, and trendy tweed jacket, she was the epitome of a capable thirty-something woman.

The fact that she was so used to being on her own only made the job of convincing her all the harder. "It doesn't have to be a real marriage," Chase continued persuasively, determined to have his way on this whether she liked it or not. "At least not in the conventional sense."

"Well, that's a relief." Merri looked at him with a mix of exasperation and cynicism in her vivid green eyes.

He regarded her seriously, aware he had a responsibility here. "Its only purpose will be to help us meet the objective."

She exhaled softly. "You becoming a father to your children."

Chase watched as she crossed her legs and clasped her delicate hands around her knee. When had she gotten so all-out beautiful? "While keeping you as the mother they know and love."

Her forehead creased. "People will talk." She pushed herself out of the swing, hips swaying provocatively as she began to pace.

Chase stayed where he was, admiring the view. "A lot less if we're married," he predicted.

Merri looked at him as if she knew that was true.

"You already asked me if I wanted to stay at the ranch with you and the kids." He stood and ambled over to join her.

Her hand encircled a post. "Temporarily. And your first instinct was to refuse."

She smelled like lavender again. Lavender and woman. "Things are different now. We have a lot more on our agenda."

"No kidding. Look, Chase, I get that we could handle this unofficially, and not get married, but...I don't want to live with someone again, without being married."

I don't want to feel used, unappreciated, not good enough.

Aware that he was scrutinizing her closely, she continued, "The problem with just living together is that it gets too complicated."

"I agree if I'm to take on the dad role—us getting hitched and becoming a 'traditional family' is the best solution."

On the surface, from a strictly practical point of view, his suggestion was workable. The ranch house had four bedrooms, only two of which were currently occupied, and comprised four thousand square feet. It was more than big enough for the two of them.

The problem was the enforced intimacy of sharing space. The fact that she was already terribly attracted to Chase and would have to be in his presence at all hours of the night and day. With vows exchanged and wedding rings on their fingers, and the whole world thinking they were husband

and wife in a very conventional sense, it would be easy to believe their union was more than a means to an end.

Once before, Merri had deluded herself into thinking that proximity plus friendship and desire would grow into something wonderful. She had ended up feeling terribly disillusioned and disappointed, when Pierce finally admitted he *didn't* really love her and didn't want to marry her. She didn't want to put her heart on the line that way again, only to be rejected in the end.

Trying not to think what Chase's steady appraisal and deep voice did to her, Merri said, "When I made the offer for you to move in, I was doing so as one extended family member to another."

He lounged against the side of the house, opposite her, his hands folded against his chest. "You're worried our relationship wouldn't stay platonic."

Well, duh. Merri stared at him, knowing a guy so virile and sexy had to have needs, too. Stubbornly, she kept her eyes locked with his even as her heart raced like a wild thing in her chest. "Aren't you?"

He shrugged, considering. "I think we're both adults and could handle whatever happens. Or doesn't."

Could they? Was she older and wiser now? More adept at limiting her emotional vulnerability? Certainly, she had lost the naivete that had made her believe in fairy-tale romance and happy endings for everyone. Merri gripped the porch railing. "So if I wanted to avoid physical intimacy…"

He squared his shoulders, suddenly looking like a knight charged with protecting his queen. "We would."

Now who was kidding whom? She hadn't had a man in heaven knew how long. The way Chase was looking at her…the place he had come from…indicated he was feeling equally deprived. Still, from a purely technical standpoint, it was a win-win solution for both of them. Especially Chase.

Up to now, he had been dealt a very bad hand in all this. Merri felt for him, and wanted to make it up to him, in whatever way she could.

"How long are we talking about?" she asked cautiously. She had lived with Pierce five years. And in the end, lost a big chunk of her prime child-bearing years to a relationship that culminated in pure heartache. Had it not been for having guardianship of the twins, she wasn't sure what she would have done.

Chase's big body began to relax. "A year? Maybe less. It all depends on how fast the twins acclimate to the idea of me being their dad."

Although the pair had been wary when they'd first greeted him, Merri knew they'd warm up to him a lot more quickly than he probably thought. "And once they do," she prodded, taking a deep breath as she searched for other pitfalls, "then what?"

He frowned, all protective male again. "If we're happy— and I have every faith we will be once we all adjust—then we stay a family."

Merri cautioned herself not to be overly optimistic about that. "And if one of us…wants more than a mere arrangement?" Such as enduring love, which had always eluded her in the past. "Then what?" she prodded.

"We can always divorce," he said simply.

Merri groaned in dismay.

He shrugged, looking ready for whatever came. "People do it all the time. The kids would adapt to that, too."

Merri drew another breath as her pulse picked up a notch. "Is that what you want?" She studied him. "A hasty marriage followed by a broken family?"

"What I want," Chase groaned, "is for this not to have happened. For Sasha and Scott not to have betrayed me. Or put either of us in this impossible situation." He grimaced.

"Since I can't undo their mistakes, I guess I want what I've always wanted. A wife who will stand by my side, and a family to come home to every night."

He paused as they both reflected on that. Merri realized they were closer in outlook than she'd thought.

"But—" Chase sighed "—that hasn't happened." He shrugged his broad shoulders. "It may never happen. Let's face it, Merri. I'm thirty-six…"

Achingly aware she needed to be realistic, too, she murmured, "I'm thirty-four." And her own fertility was waning by the day.

Their gazes met.

"Maybe it's past time to quit waiting for everything to be perfect," he said simply.

Merri thought about what he was proposing. She struggled to contain her shock. "Together," she affirmed softly.

He rubbed a hand across his jaw. "Arranged marriages have succeeded on a whole lot less."

With a beleaguered sigh of her own, Merri said, "I think this is more a marriage of convenience."

"Whatever." Briefly, irritation creased his handsome features. "You get my drift."

She did. And the most startling thing was that his suggestion didn't feel nearly as outrageous as it should. Maybe because she was disappointed in the hand fate had dealt her thus far, too. She was tired of waiting for the once-in-a-lifetime love that might never happen for her. And depriving herself of all the things she wanted in the meantime.

A contentious silence fell between them.

Merri figured as long as they were discussing this, she might as well put it all out there. She folded her arms. "Okay, let's pretend for a moment that the family part works out great. What are we going to do about sex?"

Because if she was honest, she could easily see herself

succumbing to his considerable charm. Whenever she was close to him, she felt a zing of chemistry between them.

Chase narrowed his eyes. "If it happens, it's consensual. And only with each other, as long as we're married."

"I agree anything extramarital would be a very bad idea."

He cleared his throat and folded his own arms, the motion drawing her eyes to the muscular contours of his chest. "The point is, we can't do anything about the time I've already lost with the twins. I want to be part of my kids' lives and I want to do it in such a way that doesn't rob you of any time with them." He paused and leaned toward her, further invading her personal space.

He lowered his voice. "I respect and appreciate all you have done for them thus far. I just want to be part of the process, part of the family unit. And if marriage is the only way that Judge Roy will allow me to become their co-guardian—" he paused again, and she looked straight into his mesmerizing eyes "—then I don't see any other way for me to start making up for lost time."

"We could do it unofficially."

He flashed a crooked smile. "The kids deserve better than that. They deserve a real family. And if there's even a chance that we can give them that…"

He was right. Merri released a shaky breath. "Okay. I'll do it. On one condition…."

Lines of concern bracketed his sensual lips. "And that is…?"

Merri forged ahead. "That I get something I really want out of all this, too."

"And what would that be?" He lifted a brow.

Overwhelmed by the restlessness stirring inside her, Merri angled a thumb at her chest. "What I've never had and always wanted. To carry a child inside me."

"You want to have my baby?"

Her daring surprising her, too, Merri gestured weakly. "We've already had two via medical procedure…"

Chase went still. His gaze roamed her, head to toe, then lingered on her lips. "You're asking me to impregnate you?"

He didn't have to sound so dumbfounded! "Donate sperm," Merri clarified.

Slowly, she saw her idea sink in. A corner of his mouth quirked. "I think if we decide to do this, I'd want to do it the old-fashioned way."

Me, too, if I was being completely honest. Merri suppressed a sigh. As their gazes continued to mesh, she wondered if she could really do that. Did she have it in her to love strictly as a means to an end? Amazingly enough, if the oh-so-sexy Chase Armstrong was the baby's daddy, and her lifelong dream was at stake, she imagined she could. Especially if it meant a more romantic conception for the only baby she was ever likely to have.

"All right," she allowed. "We'll…" She gulped and forced herself to go on courageously. "We'll try it the old-fashioned way." She lifted a cautioning hand. "But only when the time is right."

Chase nodded, suddenly acting more like a duty-bound medical professional than a sexually accommodating husband-to-be. "I trust you'll let me know when you're ovulating."

Merri nodded, pretending she was as relaxed about the idea of them making love as he seemed. "Sure," she said, in the most casual tone she could manage.

Another silence fell, this one more companionable. Suddenly the air was charged with hope. "In the meantime," Chase said in his typical take-charge way, "if we're really going to get hitched…how about we start taking care of the legalities?"

"You and that man—" Jessalyn pointed to Chase, still trying to comprehend what she and her twin brother had been told "—are getting married?"

Merri was still amazed at how quickly Chase had set everything up. But clearly he was a man on a mission—and the whole town seemed to have rallied around the returning local hero. "Yes." She slipped the blue velvet dress over the little girl's head, and buttoned up the back. "Chase and I are getting married."

Jessalyn sat down to shove her leotard-clad feet into her Mary Janes. "Well, then how come you're not wearing a white dress—like my Wedding Barbie doll?"

Merri turned to help Jeffrey button his shirt and slip on his tie. Quelling her own nerves, she explained gently, "Because it's not that kind of wedding. It's a small, private ceremony in the hospital chapel."

Jessalyn rose and flounced closer. "But weddings are s'posed to be in a church, not a hospital."

Merri smiled indulgently as her husband-to-be joined them. "Not always."

Looking resplendent in a dark suit, pale blue shirt and tie, Chase said, "Weddings can be anywhere you want."

Merri rose and checked her own appearance in the mirror. She had covered her navy tea-length dress with a delicate white cardigan. After much deliberation, she'd left her hair down and added pearl earrings and a necklace. The overall affect was one of understated elegance.

Aware that Chase was checking her out, too, Merri turned away from the mirror. "And the hospital chapel is kind of a church, honey—it's just a small, cozy one." *And,* she added silently, *the most logical place for the ceremony to occur on such short notice.*

Merri bent to help Jeffrey put on his jacket.

"Can we go milk the cows?" he asked, obediently sliding his hands into the navy sport coat.

"Yeah, I want to see Bessie and Blackie and Benjamen," Jessalyn declared, twirling around, her arms outstretched.

Chase sent Merri a baffled look. Knowing now was not the time to get into *that,* she focused on the twins. "We'll do that another time," she promised vaguely. Turning to Chase, she asked, "Ready?"

He nodded. Together, the four of them left the ranch house and headed for town. The hospital chaplain was waiting for them, as promised. As were their witnesses— pediatric surgeon Paige Chamberlain-McCabe and her husband, Kurt.

Paige, who'd gone to medical school with Chase, hugged him hard. "You're just full of surprises, aren't you, soldier?" she murmured.

He grinned. And keeping to the arrangement Merri and he had decided upon, which was to keep their reasons private to protect the twins from scandal, he gestured expansively. "What can I say? The heart wants what the heart wants."

Wasn't that the truth, Merri thought, as she and Chase stood before the chaplain.

The ceremony began, the words familiar, but the man beside her little more than a distant, casual friend. More than once Merri wondered if they were making a mistake. But all she had to do was look at the children, standing trustingly beside them, and know that she and Chase were doing what was best for Jeffrey and Jessalyn. And in the end, wasn't that all that really mattered? Seeing that the kids didn't suffer for mistakes made by others years ago?

Finally, with vows exchanged and rings on their fingers,

the ceremony was complete. "Chase, you may kiss your bride," the chaplain said.

And he did.

CHASE HADN'T MEANT TO GIVE Merri more than a peck on the lips, but with everyone standing there, watching, the adults with more than a little skepticism, he decided to take the plunge and give it his all.

Wrapping one arm around her shoulders, his other her waist, he drew her against him. She lifted her face and he lowered his. As contact was made, potent desire roared through him. She caught her breath and gave a little sound that was half murmur, half moan. Her unbidden response compelled him to draw her closer still, allowing the passion zinging through him to dictate the pressure and the pace. Only the fact that they had an audience made him put on the brakes.

Slowly, he released her. Merri stared up at him, dazed. He felt the same shock and amazement.

Kurt cleared his throat. "Wow," Chase's old pal murmured. "This is for real."

It certainly felt that way, Chase realized. He just wasn't sure if the chemistry between Merri and him was going to make things easier or harder in the days and months ahead.

A hospital volunteer appeared in the doorway of the chapel. "There you are, Dr. Armstrong! I heard you were here. These came for you!" The pink-coated woman rushed forward, a big autumn floral arrangement clasped in her arms. In the center was a large envelope with Chase's name written on it.

Jeffrey tugged on Chase's jacket. "Is that a present?"

"Open it!" Jessalyn demanded, crowding in, too.

Chase broke the seal, and pulled out a card.

It featured an eight-by-ten glossy photograph, not the

kind that any groom should be receiving on his wedding day. As his "wife" looked over his shoulder, she seemed to agree.

"Wow," Merri murmured in shock.

Half a dozen young women were gathered in what looked to be a field hospital. All were clad in desert fatigues, boots and T-shirts. All were holding signs.

"What does it say?" Jessalyn demanded.

"Yeah, Mommy, read it," Jeffrey chimed in.

"Well, it says 'We love you, Chase. Miss you already! Can't believe you actually left us! Holidays are meant to be shared! Texas equals home and home is where the heart is.' And last but not least…" Merri read the sign held up by a particularly beautiful brunette. "'We hate that you left us, but…see you soon!'"

She turned to Chase. "Got quite a cast of admirers there," she drawled.

He grinned good-naturedly. "They like to tease me, that's for sure."

As long as teasing was all they were doing, Merri thought irritably.

"Where should I put them?" the volunteer asked. "Your office…?"

"Sure you don't want to take them home with us?" Merri asked tartly.

"Actually," Chase said, keeping the photo, and giving back the floral arrangement, "why don't you set this in the lobby? That way, everyone can enjoy it."

"Good idea." Smiling, the volunteer walked out, vase in hand.

Kate Marten-McCabe came in with a young nursing student at her side. Head of the hospital grief counseling services for the last thirty years, Kate was beautiful, kind and direct to a fault. "Chase, Merri, good to see you." She knelt by the twins with a charismatic smile. "I need to talk to the bride and groom. And it's grown-up talk." Kate made a face. The kids giggled and wrinkled their noses back at her. "How would you two like to go down to the playroom in pediatrics for a few minutes? We have a lot of fun toys, and Sally here—" Kate pointed to the nursing student "—would love to show them to you."

When Jessalyn and Jeffrey nodded, Kate looked at the newlyweds. "Is this okay with you?"

Aware that whatever this entailed was definitely not for children's ears, they assented. After the kids took off with Sally, Chase and Merri followed Kate into her office.

The grief counselor sat down behind her desk. "Luke Carrigan, the chief of staff, asked me to speak with you. There's no easy way to say this, so I'll be blunt. He heard about the marriage and he's concerned."

Chase frowned, clearly taken aback. "Because...?"

Compassion lit Kate's kind eyes. "You've just returned from a very stressful situation. And he wants to make sure you're not suffering from any kind of post-traumatic stress disorder."

Chase blinked, a little stunned by the assertion. He reached over and took Merri's hand, letting her know he was more than capable of handling this concern on their behalf. "I was never wounded. Or captured."

With a cajoling smile, Kate continued, "But you dealt with people who were.... And there are family deaths you never really had a chance to deal with, all of which could combine to make you do things that you wouldn't normally."

"I didn't marry Merri out of any reaction to that," Chase said, confident as ever.

The grief counselor relaxed. "I'm glad to hear it."

And yet, Merri thought, Kate obviously continued to sense something was up.

Eager to end this line of questioning, Merri slid her hand into Chase's and sent him a warning glance. "I think she's concerned because no one knew you and I were thinking along these lines, Chase."

Kate nodded soberly, picking up where Merri left off. "You have to admit it's a shock to the community at large."

Aggravation twisted the corners of his lips. "It's also no one else's business," he stated in a flat, implacable tone.

Suddenly feeling as if she were dealing with a bull in a china shop, Merri continued to play peacemaker. She stood, dragging Chase along with her. "I—we—understand where you and Dr. Carrigan are coming from, Kate, and believe me, we appreciate your concern."

Merri flashed a reassuring smile, while Chase played along, wrapping an arm about her waist. "But there's really no need to worry." Drawing strength from his warmth, she took another bolstering breath. "Chase and I know we did the right thing in getting married. Not just for the two of us and our future, but for the twins." She paused, letting her words sink in. "The kids need a daddy. And Chase and I are going to see that they get the complete family they deserve."

CHASE'S EXPRESSION WAS maddeningly inscrutable as they left the hospital counseling center. "You didn't have to defend us," he stated.

Merri flushed self-consciously. "Uh, yeah, I did."

"How come?" he asked.

Aware this was a conversation that should not be overheard, she ducked into a small alcove in the painted, cement-block corridor. Defiantly, she lifted her chin. "Laramie County is a small, close-knit community, remember?"

He folded his arms across his chest and shot her a laser-sharp look.

With her back against the cool hospital wall, she ignored the sexual heat radiating from him, and lowered her voice to a whisper. "Everyone watches out for everyone else here."

He shrugged and leaned in closer yet, dropping his voice, too. "So?" he prodded in a sexy murmur.

Merri drank in the crisp, masculine fragrance emanating from him. "So people are understandably concerned and confused...given how fast this has all come about." She drew a breath, reassuring herself that despite the impact of their post-nuptial kiss, they were in no real danger of hooking up in the near future. Both of them were much too sensible. "You don't agree?"

He braced his hands on his hips, his expression becoming even more guarded. "I think they should mind their own business. We're adults, after all."

She forced herself to glance away. "Who, you have to admit, are now acting very mysteriously."

He bent down, caging her with his arms and lowered his face until their mouths were an inch apart. He lifted a strand of hair from her cheek and tucked it behind her ear. Came even nearer, so their bodies were touching and she could feel the heat emanating from his. "So what you're saying is we've got some convincing to do if people are going to believe this marriage is for real," he proposed silkily.

Out of the corner of her eye, Merri saw people lingering at the far end of the corridor, near the elevators.

"No." She swallowed as he cupped her face in his hands. "That's not what I said at all."

"Too bad," Chase murmured, the amorous glint in his eyes letting her know he planned to make their union as realistic and convincing as possible, for all the doubting Thomases in the vicinity. After all, he knew as well as she did that word of the incident would quickly spread, through the hospital grapevine, then the community at large.

His lips touched hers in a sweet, chaste kiss. "Because it's what *I* say," he vowed, planting a hotly possessive kiss on her mouth.

Merri knew it was all for show. As his lips moved slowly and sensually over hers, she swore that she wasn't going to kiss him back, but instead would let him do all the work.

It was a good plan. A very safe, intelligent way of resisting him. Unfortunately it backfired big-time. Before even a millisecond went by, her lips parted beneath the persuasive pressure of his. Her knees weakened and her heart rate skyrocketed. Succumbing, she wreathed her arms around his neck and kissed him back, melting against him.

And that was when the polite throat-clearing sounded, followed by rapid footsteps. Breathlessly, Chase and Merri moved apart, only to see Jessalyn and Jeffrey skid to a halt on the shiny linoleum floor.

Then came the confused, indignant demand, "Mommy! Why are you kissing that man!"

REMINDED THAT ALTHOUGH Chase might secretly be the kids' biological father, they barely knew who he was—a fact that would quickly have to be rectified—Merri flushed. "We'll talk about it at home." She took the children's hands and told Sally, "Thank you for watching over them."

"No problem," the nursing student replied cheerfully. "And congratulations, you two! Everyone is saying this came out of left field, but the way the doc was kissing you just now? No way!" she proclaimed. She pointed to Merri and Chase before heading off to resume her duties. "That's definitely the real deal."

"Mommy! You didn't answer my question! Why were you kissing him? Again!" Jessalyn said in annoyance.

"Because we're married and married people kiss sometimes. Especially—" Merri elbowed Chase "—when they are trying to make a point."

He leaned down to whisper in her ear, "Hey, it worked, didn't it?"

To rev her up, maybe. And start more gossip.

Jeffrey and Jessalyn looked at each other, perplexed. Clearly, they didn't know what to make of this. "So what now?" Chase asked as he and Merri left the hospital, kids in tow.

"I still want to go milk the cows," Jessalyn insisted.

"Me, too," Jeffrey chimed in.

Chase waited for Merri to decide. "Actually, we do have to get back to the ranch," she said eventually.

"Hurrah!" Jeffrey and Jessalyn cried in unison.

"I thought you got rid of the beef cattle years ago." Chase held open the car door for the kids.

"I had to. Scott and Sasha went deep into debt to pay for their fertility treatments, and it was the only way to settle the estate so it could get through probate."

Chase didn't look surprised to learn his brother and sister-in-law had gravely mismanaged the ranch. "And you've just leased the land since, for crops and grazing?"

Nodding, Merri leaned in to help Jessalyn fasten her safety harness. "Initially, all I did was allow others to plant alfalfa, hay and corn on the farmable land, and rotate the cattle on other parts, for grazing."

Chase did the same for Jeffrey. "And that brought in more than enough to pay the mortgage and the taxes and the upkeep on the property?"

"As well as a small salary for me."

"But...?" he prodded, sensing there was more.

Merri climbed into the passenger seat. "Eventually, I realized I needed to build something of my own for me and the kids, and take a more active part in the running of the ranch." She tugged her dress down over her knees. "Which is when I converted the barn on the south part of the property to a milking operation, hired one full-time hand to help me manage it and bought a dozen Jersey cows and a dozen Guernseys."

Chase did a double take. "You're turning the Broken Arrow Ranch into a dairy farm?"

"Uh, yeah....I am."

His jaw tautened. "You never mentioned it in any of your letters."

That's because I knew you wouldn't approve. "Hmm. Didn't I?"

He made a face.

"The cows are really cute," Jessalyn interjected from her booster seat. "Some are brown and white and some are black and white...."

"I like it when they moo," Jeffrey declared.

Chase continued gaping at Merri as if she were a complete and utter fool. She refused to let his skepticism get her down. "It's a good thing," she promised, sure about this decision even if she wasn't so certain about others. Cheerfully, she predicted, "And it will be even better in a few years, when we get the dairy operation expanded to quadruple the size."

MERRI HADN'T BEEN KIDDING, Chase noted thirty minutes later when all four of them had changed into "ranch clothes," hopped in the pickup truck and headed for the south side of the Broken Arrow Ranch. Just as she had claimed, there were twenty-four cows pastured outside the big barn. All were big, robust, surprisingly handsome animals. Most were heading slowly for the barn door as the truck approached.

"The cows like to come in all on their own!" Jessalyn announced.

"But if they don't, Mutt—the doggie—will help Slim get the cows inside the barn, so they can get hooked up," Jeffrey added helpfully.

"The cows know when it's time to be milked, so they head for the barn," Merri explained.

Chase parked in the gravel area and everyone got out.

A tall, thin cowboy in his mid-fifties came out of the barn, with a border collie at his heels. The gray-haired hired hand tipped his hat at Merri before glancing at Chase. "I expect you want to have a look around," he drawled, with the respect due one of the original Armstrongs.

Did he? Chase wondered.

Finding out what Merri had been doing to the place was his worst nightmare. He was stunned no one had mentioned it. But maybe they'd figured—rightly so—that it was going to be a sore subject with him.

Chase tipped his hat back to Slim, a cowboy he recalled meeting at the barbecue in his honor. "May as well," he grumbled.

Clasping the children's hands, Merri led the way inside the sparkling, clean barn.

Chase was stunned to see twenty-four stalls, and plenty of stainless-steel, state-of-the-art milking equipment with hoses running to a big steel vat.

Merri murmured with pride, "I joined a co-op dairy that supplies organic milk to a big grocery store chain. Every day a truck comes in and takes it to the processing plant, for ultrahigh-temperature processing and packaging."

"I don't like the truck," Jessalyn complained, covering her ears. "It's too noisy."

"But we like watching the cows get milked," Jeffrey said.

As the bovines were ushered into the stalls, they were

hooked up to the milking machines. For all the activity, the barn was surprisingly quiet and peaceful.

Chase's cell phone rang.

He stepped outside to take the call, then walked back in to let Merri know the latest. "That was Liz Cartwright Anderson. She got us on Judge Roy's docket for tomorrow afternoon at four. We're the last case the judge is going to hear before the Thanksgiving break."

A fact, Chase thought happily, that put them one step closer to his ultimate goal: to have this family officially his.

Chapter Three

"You know what I think?" Judge Priscilla Roy said after listening to Chase and Merri's joint request for guardianship. In her black robe, glasses perched on the edge of her nose, the dark-haired justice cut an imposing figure as she glared at Chase. "None of what is going on here today, or what happened yesterday in the hospital chapel, has anything to do with the kind of unconditional love and commitment needed for a successful marriage, never mind a stable family unit."

She was right about that, Merri thought. Their union wasn't about the feelings she and Chase had for each other.

"I think you're just doing this to provide access to the children slash heirs and get back control of the family ranch."

Merri blinked. *What?*

"Your Honor. There has been no request from Mr. Armstrong for control of the children's estate," Liz interjected with lawyerly calm.

Judge Roy waved her hand, then drew her glasses farther down the bridge of her nose and peered at Chase. "Don't tell me you're happy about what happened to the ranch you grew up on. Armstrongs and the Broken Arrow have always raised beef cattle. Not dairy cows."

"That's true," Chase admitted with admirable candor.

"What's happened there would not have been my choice. But I do understand." He turned to glance at Merri. "My wife had to raise these kids on her own and take care of the property. She's done the best she could under the circumstances."

Unmoved, Judge Roy continued, "But you could do better?"

Chase lifted his hands. "I'm a surgeon."

Sternly, the judge commanded, "Answer the question, please."

He released an exasperated breath and looked at her, squaring his shoulders deliberately. "Yes. I think I could do better. But that's not the point, Your Honor."

"Actually, Mr. and Mrs. Armstrong, I think that is exactly the point. Mr. Armstrong is back in town and wants what was previously denied him by his mother's estate—control of the ranch and its assets, which are currently held in trust for the children. To get that, he would have to be coguardian of the kids." Priscilla Roy paused meaningfully. "And to achieve that, at least in my courtroom, he has to be married to Merri Duncan. Which he has managed in very short order, with no prior courtship, at least that anyone in the county seems to know about."

Merri didn't know what they could say to that, without breaking the promise she and Chase had made to each other to keep the twins' biological origins private and hence protect the children from scandal. It was bad enough that they'd been orphaned at eight weeks of age, without making Scott and Sasha out to be conniving liars.

Thank heavens the twins didn't understand any of this. At four and a half, they simply wanted Merri to be their mommy, and hopefully soon, for Chase to be their daddy.

"Judge," Liz interrupted, "if I may... I have spoken at length with my clients. They both want what is best for these children. Jeffrey and Jessalyn need a father and a mother, and my clients are willing to make the necessary sacrifices and work together to provide that."

Judge Roy looked at Merri. "An early Christmas gift?"

Wary of making a mistake that would put them in even deeper trouble, she admitted cautiously, "Something like that."

"Correct me if I'm wrong. You worked as a wedding planner before settling back in Laramie County?"

Merri nodded. "That's true."

Judge Roy rocked back in her chair. "And isn't that a romantic profession?"

Merri winced. "It's a profession that provides romance. I don't know how romantic it is for the planner at the end of the day." She sighed. "Weddings can be very stressful. And a lot of time, the days leading up to the ceremony are anything but romantic."

The justice pushed her glasses back into place. "So in other words, your work left you jaded."

Merri shrugged and risked a tiny glance at Chase, who stood beside her, sober and strong. "Maybe. A little." As had her personal experiences with relationships. "But also exceedingly practical." She paused, searching for the right words. "I do want what is best for the children. And I think having Chase in their lives, as their dad, will provide that." It was certainly better than splitting the children up, one night at her place, one night at his.... Which was the only other fair alternative.

"Okay." Judge Roy sat back, folded her hands on the desk. "You've convinced me to give you a chance. But that is all it is. An opportunity to prove that your marriage is a real one, not a sham, and what you are proposing is in the best interest of the twins. If I find out you're misleading this court in any way, if this marriage is simply a means to an end, I'll remove you both as guardians."

Remove? Merri blinked in shock.

Judge Roy turned to her clerk. "Schedule another hearing, for January 3." She banged her gavel, signaling their hearing had come to an end.

Stunned, Merri left the courtroom with Chase and Liz, as the next case was called. Their lawyer guided them down the hall to a spot where they could talk privately.

"Would the judge really do that?" Merri asked, her voice wobbling as badly as her knees. Clapping a hand over heart, she sank down on the closest wooden bench. "Take the kids away from us?"

"It's within Judge Roy's power. But she's not going to do that, as long as this is a genuine attempt to build a loving, supportive family that will benefit all of you in the long run."

"It is," Chase said firmly, with laudable assurance. "Merri and I will make this work."

Merri only wished she felt as confident.

"So much for our plans to divorce if things don't work out," she murmured as the two of them walked to the parking lot. She still felt shaky and at a loss. Chase, on the other hand, looked more confident than ever.

"Judge Roy had a point. Nothing good was ever accomplished with one foot out the door."

Merri knew the words were truer than she wished. Still... "I'm scared."

He caught her to him as they reached the car. "Don't be," he murmured with both hands on her shoulders. He looked deep into her eyes. "We're two very strong people, who want only the best for the kids. We'll find a way to make it work."

Chase was as good as his word. He was there to help, with dinner and baths and story time. Jeffrey and Jessalyn still regarded him with wariness, but they were slowly warming to him, Merri could tell. As was evidenced by the last question of the day, as they were being tucked in for the night.

"Is Chase going to be our daddy...now that you two are married?" Jessalyn asked.

Merri looked at Chase. He waited, leaving the answer up to her. They hadn't broached the subject yet, because they hadn't wanted to rush the kids. "Yes, this makes him your daddy," Merri said, with as much ease as she could muster.

"Is that okay with you?" Chase asked.

Jessalyn and Jeffrey exchanged looks. Two lower lips slid out truculently. "No," Jeffrey said.

"We don't want a daddy right now," Jessalyn added.

Chase's expression was inscrutable, but Merri could tell from the faint sheen in his eyes that he was crushed. As was she. "Why not?" she asked the kids, when she found her voice.

"Because we already got a mommy, so we don't need a daddy," Jessalyn explained.

"It's okay," Chase assured them, seeming to understand that he had upset the equanimity of the household.

"You can change your minds anytime," Merri felt compelled to add.

Jeffrey sighed and hugged his teddy bear tightly. "We're not going to."

Jessalyn nodded in agreement. And that, it seemed, was that.

"SORRY THEY WEREN'T MORE cooperative," Merri said as she and Chase went down the stairs together.

"They'll warm up," he predicted.

Merri hoped so. Thanks to Judge Roy's ultimatum, they didn't have a lot of time to make this work.

Unfortunately, Chase had an early call at the hospital. So the twins didn't see him at all the next morning before preschool.

"Try a lot of short visits," Merri's friend Paige said, when she talked to her later that morning. Paige was not only a dedicated pediatrician, but also an experienced mother of demanding triplets. "It will help the kids get used to Chase and vice versa, and put a lot less pressure on all of them."

Deciding it was good advice, Merri stopped by the hospital complex, after picking up the kids from school.

"How come we're going to the hospital?" Jessalyn asked.

"I don't want another shot," Jeffrey whimpered, holding his hand over his thigh.

Paige held open the door to the hospital annex, where all the physician offices were located. "You're not going to get one today. You already had your flu shots last month, remember?"

Jeffrey rubbed his thigh in memory. "That's why I don't want another one."

"So how come we're here, if we're not going to the doctor?" Jessalyn persisted, pausing to study the festive turkey and cornucopia display taped outside the pediatric services suite.

Merri took the children's hands and pressed on. "I thought we'd surprise Chase and see if he'd like to have lunch with us in the cafeteria."

More frowns. "I'd rather go to the Dairy Barn," Jessalyn said with a pout.

Merri paused outside the general surgery suite. "Another time," she promised.

She ushered the children in, only to be told by the receptionist, "You just missed him. He went down to the cafeteria to grab a bite to eat."

"Perfect!" Merri smiled and ushered the children back

out into the hall. Not surprisingly, they grumbled and dragged their heels all the way to the cafeteria.

Chase had already gone through the line. Tray in hand, he was searching for a seat when he saw them. He flashed a devastating smile, set his tray on a table for four and strode toward them.

He was looking more handsome than ever in blue surgical scrubs and a white doctor's coat, and Merri felt her heart quiver in response. She knew this wasn't a real marriage in the traditional sense, but at the moment, it felt as if it were.

Aware that all eyes were on them, she beamed at him. "Hey."

Still smiling, Chase pressed a quick, casual kiss to her temple, then leaned down to do the same to the kids.

Instead of welcoming the gesture, they both shrank back, out of reach. The twins clung to Merri, hiding their faces in the fabric of her wool trousers.

"Can we go home now?" Jeffrey's voice was muffled against her leg.

Merri patted his shoulder reassuringly. "Let's have some lunch first, okay?"

The little boy was about to protest when a loud cheer went up behind them. Squeals of delight were followed by a chorus of "There he is!" "What a sight for sore eyes!" "Handsome as always, Dr. Heartbreaker!"

Dr. Heartbreaker?

Merri turned, coming face-to-face with the half-dozen young women from Chase's photo. They were clad in desert-hued camouflage pants, jackets and form-fitting beige T-shirts, and were all incredibly glad to see Chase. From the welcoming expression on her now husband's face, he was equally thrilled to see them.

En masse, the women streamed toward him. And one after another, with everyone in the hospital cafeteria looking on, they greeted Chase with more whoops and hollers and heartfelt hugs.

"What are you-all doing here?" he asked, beaming as if he had just won the lottery.

And maybe he had.

One of the ladies flashed a megawatt smile. "You said we could visit anytime and you'd put us up!"

"So when we all unexpectedly got a month's leave and decided to go on a road trip, we figured we'd take you up on it," a striking brunette added, going on tiptoe to give Chase another long, lingering hug. She drew back, the name-necklace at her throat glittering, and with an air of feminine possessiveness punched on his broad shoulder playfully. "Besides, what's a holiday without our favorite guy?"

Okay. Enough was enough, especially with a big chunk of the hospital visitors and staff looking on, absorbing every word.

"Or his family," Merri interjected sweetly, asserting herself once again.

The women all turned to look at her and the children.

Abruptly recalling his manners, Chase stepped back. Drawing Merri and the kids around him, he said, "Ladies, I'd like you to meet my wife, Merri, and our kids, Jeffrey and Jessalyn."

Our kids. Merri liked the sound of that almost as much as the sound of *my wife.*

"Wife?" the women echoed in shock.

The brunette with the name necklace—Starr—stepped forward. "Kids?" she demanded. "Since when?"

"Don't tell us you were married all along, you heartbreaker!" the freckled redhead said.

"Actually, we just got married yesterday," Merri told them.

Six brows furrowed in confusion.

Chase lifted a palm, not about to go into it there with the entire hospital cafeteria crowd still watching. "It's a long story," he said mildly.

"Fortunately," the striking brunette, Starr, said with a playful moue, "we've got all the time in the world to hear it." She insinuated herself between Chase and Merri, snuggled up to his side and gazed up at him adoringly. "That is, if you're still as good as your word, Chase Armstrong, and intend to put us all up for the Thanksgiving holiday, Texas-style."

Chapter Four

"It's too much to ask."

Maybe for a casual friend, but for a presumably loving wife? Merri wondered.

"You don't have to do this," Chase told her, after his army buddies had promised to meet up with him when he got off work at five-thirty.

To Merri's relief, the bevy of attractive women had gone, en masse, to the shops on Main Street, to purchase some genuine "Texas" duds for their three-day stay. The twins were seated at a table by the window, happily chowing down on some ice cream, while Merri and Chase talked quietly, just out of earshot.

"I'll figure something else out," he promised, sipping his coffee.

Merri leaned her back against the cafeteria wall, glad most of the lunch crowd and staff had dispersed. She turned to Chase, feeling the heat of his gaze like a physical caress. "Really?"

He didn't take his eyes off her. "Really."

She ran a hand through her hair, suddenly feeling a little too aware of her hunky new husband. "Where are your friends going to go? It's the Wednesday before Thanksgiving. Every hotel room in a hundred-mile radius has been booked for months."

A conflicted glimmer appeared in Chase's eyes. Obviously, he hadn't thought about the impact the holiday would have on hotel room availability in rural west Texas. He did, however, seem to realize that Merri was suddenly feeling as if she had been relegated to seventh-wheel status, in the pecking order of go-getting females who'd traveled thousands of miles to be with him.

His handsome features tightened in resignation. "I'm sorry, Merri. You and I should be focused on the kids now, getting them adjusted to the changes in our lives. Instead…" He paused, shook his head then sent her a beseeching glance.

They had houseguests.

Lots of very attractive, very smitten female houseguests.

Chase continued, "When I issued the standing invitation to everyone in my unit, I wasn't married."

Merri knew the appearance of his army buddies was unexpected—although maybe she and Chase should have gotten a clue from the holiday gift basket and card, and all the signs the women were holding up in the photo.

But that only made it a tiny bit better. Because Chase was right…it would be best if they could focus on the kids—and being married—without an audience of half a dozen very interested admirers.

Still, it was the holiday season, a time of thanks and giving. And these were friends and colleagues who had served in the military field hospital alongside Chase. Merri put her emotions aside, dug deep and called up the generosity the situation required.

She reached out and touched his arm gently. "It's okay, Chase. Really." She looked into his eyes, so he would know she meant what she said from the bottom of her heart. "It's only for a couple of nights, and we have room at the ranch—

if everyone doubles up and two people volunteer to sleep on sofas."

Chase's brow furrowed as he calculated, same as Merri. There were two guest rooms, two sofas, one master suite… and eight adults.

"Obviously, you'll have to sleep in my room temporarily." Merri stepped back slightly. Thinking about what it would be like to share the sheets with him, she struggled to control a self-conscious flush.

Chuckling, he took her hand. Warmth spread throughout her body as his fingers engulfed hers. "There's always the barn…."

Merri's throat went dry as she gazed up into his mischievous eyes. "Hilarious," she muttered, then returned to the matter at hand. "But like it or not, we'll have to sleep together as long as we have company. Otherwise people will speculate more than they already are."

"How do you know they're speculating?" he asked in surprise.

Seriously? Merri rolled her eyes in exasperation. A hot development like the marriage was probably all over the hospital and town grapevines. "Did you not see the looks we were getting in the cafeteria when your lady friends arrived?"

"Uh…" Chase shrugged his broad shoulders, looking every bit the clueless male. "Not really…"

"What about before that?" Merri pressed. "When we said hello and the kids were anything but happy to see their new dad?"

A look of hurt flashed in Chase's eyes, then disappeared. That he apparently did recall, all too acutely, and Merri's heart went out to him. He had already missed so much. First steps, first words. All those Christmases and birthdays. The first day of preschool. Through no fault of his own.

His expression sobered, becoming all the more sincere. "I think you're being too sensitive," he countered softly. "People understand we just got married and are in an adjustment period here."

She studied his big, scrub-clad frame, deciding he was way too sexy in whatever he wore. Way too masculine and capable and kind. Aware that she could fall hard for Chase if she wasn't careful—and she intended to be careful, particularly with a bevy of female admirers suddenly in the picture. Merri folded her arms in front of her. "Maybe people also understand a lot more than we'd like them to—which is why everyone is so skeptical when they look at us."

What if they couldn't fool his friends? Merri worried nervously.

Or anyone else, for that matter. What would Judge Roy do if she concluded that Merri and Chase were just scamming the court, as a means to an end? Laramie County was a close-knit community. Sooner or later, everyone knew everyone else's business. Or at least most of it.

People certainly knew who loved whom, and who only pretended to care....

Zeroing in on her nervousness, Chase cupped her arms reassuringly and leaned closer. "We're going to make this work, Merri."

His hands felt as warm and strong as the rest of him looked. Shivering at his touch, she murmured distractedly, "You keep saying that." How could he have so much faith?

His smile was slow and sure. "I keep meaning it, too."

Inhaling the mixture of hospital antiseptic and his favorite bath soap rising from his skin, Merri edged back. "I'm beginning to see that," she returned softly. And although she didn't share his hope and faith—her past experiences had drained them out of her—she couldn't help but admire his bravura.

A tenuous silence fell.

Abruptly, Merri noticed that people were staring. Again. Including the twins, who had just about finished their ice cream.

Reluctantly, Chase relinquished his hold on her and dropped his hands to his sides. "So where are you and the kids off to next?" he inquired.

She shrugged, her emotions in turmoil once again. "Depends. What do you want to do about dinner? With—" she cleared her throat "—all our *guests?*"

Chase scrubbed his hand across his jaw, considering. "I could pick up Sonny's Barbecue on the way home."

Now, that was helpful! "Sounds perfect, thank you." Merri smiled. "Meanwhile, the kids and I will head to the grocery store to stock up on essentials for our guests, plus all the ingredients for the cooking I have to do tonight."

He studied her face, clearly puzzled, and Merri realized she should have warned him about that. "The community center Thanksgiving dinner is early tomorrow afternoon. It's a potluck. The kids and I attend every year. And this year I'm tasked with bringing ten crowd-size sweet potato casseroles."

"So it really isn't a good time to have all that company," Chase concluded with a frown.

Merri appreciated his consideration and clasped his biceps gently. "It's really nice that your army buddies got to come back to the States for the holidays. Even better that you all have a chance to be together for a few days." She released her hold, stepped back and tossed him the confident smile that had gotten her through many a challenging situation. "I'll do my best to make sure they feel welcome."

MERRI MADE GOOD ON HER promise to Chase. And as she got to know the women, found she had more in common with them than she first thought. Addie had grown up on a farm. Nissa had twin brothers. Davita's sister was a wedding planner. Harmony had never known her dad. Polly had entrepreneurial dreams. And Starr had the biggest crush of all on Chase.

A fact that seemed to go unnoticed by Merri's dashing new husband. Which made the queries that came up, as soon as the twins were sound asleep in bed, expected, if not exactly welcome.

"So," Starr said, sauntering over to stand next to Chase. "Tell us how the two of you met and fell in love."

All eyes turned to Chase, who finished building the fire in the hearth, then straightened casually. "I don't recall an exact moment. It was more an awareness that we had a connection—"

That is, Jessalyn and Jeffrey, Merri thought.

"—and that this was what we wanted to do," Chase finished calmly.

Faces fell in disappointment. It hadn't been a very romantic rendition, Merri acknowledged, although what he'd revealed *had* been completely truthful.

Smiling brightly as Chase came toward her, she added a few facts of her own. "Chase and I both grew up in Laramie County, so we've always known each other. Although not that well when we were growing up, since he was four years ahead of me in school."

"When did that change?" Davita asked curiously.

Chase sat on the arm of Merri's chair, took her hand in his. He turned her palm up and traced the lifeline. "When my brother and her sister became engaged. We were thrown together a lot in the months leading up to their marriage."

"But you never mentioned her," Starr protested.

Addie gave the striking brunette a reproving look, then turned back with a smile. "I think we all know that Chase is a guy who plays his cards close to his chest. Especially in the romantic arena."

He stood and, all protective male, pulled Merri to her feet beside him. "You-all must be exhausted," he said to their houseguests. "What do you say we turn in? Tomorrow morning will be here before we know it."

Ten minutes later, Merri and Chase were in the master bedroom, hearing just a few low voices as doors opened and closed. Merri slipped into the adjacent bath. She emerged five minutes later in blue-and-white polka dot pajama pants and a gray henley.

To her surprise, Chase was already undressed, down to a pair of boxers and a T-shirt. His legs and arms were as sinewy and masculine as she had imagined. "That's all you're wearing?" she asked.

Laugh lines crinkled at the corners of his eyes. "Be thankful," he teased, pulling at the neck of his T-shirt. "It's more than I usually do. But you're right… With the kids and company around, I'm probably going to have to invest in pajamas."

Merri wasn't sure the image of him in cotton pajama pants would be any less sexy. Especially if he purchased the kind that would ride low on his lean hips.

Oblivious to the sensual nature of her thoughts, he sauntered into the bathroom, toothbrush in hand. Merri watched his retreating backside wistfully.

He was so darn buff, so hotly male. And she should not be objectifying him this way.…

To distract herself, Merri climbed into bed and started to make a list in her head. She had so much to do with Christmas less than a month away!

By the time Chase returned, she had switched off the light. The to-do list had grown to a daunting length.

Luckily for him, the combination of a night-light and

the moonlight streaming in through cracks in the blinds gave him enough illumination to maneuver without bumping into anything.

As he neared, she decided lying on her back did not seem like the wisest choice. So Merri shifted to a less vulnerable position and propped her head on her upraised palm. "What are we going to do?" she whispered, when he finally settled beside her.

Chase turned onto his side, so they were lying there face-to-face. He surveyed her with a guileless grin. "Now?"

Merri tugged her attention away from the powerful muscles of his shoulders. She shouldn't be noticing, but hallelujah, he had a nice chest. Nice butt. Nice legs. And arms... She licked her suddenly dry lips, glad those boxers of his were loose fitting and an opaque army-green. "About all the questions," she said, trying in vain to get her thoughts—and her libido—back on track.

He continued to regard her nonchalantly, lying there in her bed, looking as relaxed as could be. "We'll do what we've already been doing," he murmured. "Distract. Divert. And not really answer. At least not all the way." He rolled over onto his back and folded his hands behind his head. Unfortunately, the action only served to show her how flat his stomach, and how well-endowed the rest of him, was.

"I don't think that's going to work." She snuggled more deeply into the sheets, wishing it didn't feel so cozy, lying here with him. "Not if they're as curious and probing as they have been."

"Sure it will." He turned his head and flashed her another sexy grin. "It will if we keep stonewalling."

Merri rolled onto her back, too. For several minutes they lay there in the semidarkness, side by side. Yet Merri could tell by the set of his shoulders and the sound of his breathing that he was no more inclined to go to sleep than she was.

Finally, Chase reached over and ran a hand along her forearm. "Is that the only thing bothering you?"

Her skin tingling from the compassionate touch, Merri turned her glance away from the shadows on the ceiling. If she was going to be one hundred percent honest, she'd have to admit she was a tiny bit jealous, having all those adoring females there with them. Not sure what that said about her, and certainly not about to admit she was already feeling so wifely and possessive, she rolled away from him, and retorted in a muffled voice, "I don't like being put on the spot."

He hooked an arm around her waist and pulled her back until her shoulders were pressed against the hard, unyielding muscles of his chest, and her bottom was nestled against his abdomen and thighs. The action was meant to comfort; she could feel it in the platonic nature of his grasp. Yet it was a very sexy, provocative embrace just the same.

"Neither do I," he whispered in her ear, with a lot more kindness and understanding than she would have expected. Was this the type of husband he was going to be? Gentle and affectionate? Up till now, she had put him firmly in the friends category, knowing that one day soon, when they were ready to make a baby, she'd have to move him into the friends-with-benefits group.

But this suddenly felt a lot more emotionally seductive. And hence, dangerous in the lose-your-heart-to-a-man-you-know-will-really-love-you kind of way.

Pushing aside her senseless fairy-tale wishes, Merri listened to the rest of what Chase had on his mind.

"But as you said earlier," he reminded her casually, "my friends are only going to be here for a couple more days."

Merri shut her eyes and told herself that this was not desire she was feeling. Though their thighs were pressed together, his hips were a safe distance away.

Pressing his warm chest against her back, he was comforting her, in a husbandly sort of way, not seducing. She closed her eyes, wondering if he was as aroused as she was beginning to be.

Merri shifted her free arm across her breasts. A few more days? "That's still long enough for your gal pals to continue the inquisition." Which could put them in an even more awkward position than they were now, sharing her way-too-small bed, pretending it was a normal, expected event.

Grasping her shoulder, Chase turned her so she was lying flat on her back once again. He positioned himself a safe distance away, propped his head on his hand and stared down into her face, looking as if he wanted nothing more than to kiss her again. This time, strictly for them and no one else.

There was only one thing she could think of doing, when he looked at her that way. The problem was that if she gave in to the surge of recklessness she felt, all her carefully constructed barriers would fall away. At this moment, theirs was a marriage in name only. For both their sakes, she needed to remember that, as did he.

Chase shrugged, his own desire under a lot better control than hers. "Well, then, guess we'll all just have to stay busy, won't we?"

"Speaking of that…" She swallowed, noting the sudden parched feeling in her throat, and struggled not to think of how "being busy" making love with him might feel.

Because that just wasn't going to happen.

At least not in the next couple of days—since a pack of way-too-observant females had systematically taken over the house.

No. When it finally happened, it would just be the two of them. Alone in this house. No distractions. No time limits. No having to be careful or quiet.…

Aware how all this trying-to-not-be-turned-on was actually arousing her even more, Merri jerked in an uneven breath. "Did I tell you I'm on duty for the milking tomorrow?"

Obviously enjoying how flustered she'd become, he tilted his head and gave her a cocky grin. "No."

Glad to talk about work, Merri replied, "Traditionally, Slim has Thanksgiving Day and Friday off, and then he does Saturday and Sunday for me."

"Want me to help?" Chase asked, gallant as ever.

Oh, Lord, if ever there was a knight in shining armor…

"No." Nor did she want him to forget everything they had previously agreed to, and make hot, wild, unrestrained love to her. Here and now, company be damned.

Shaking off the image of her stretched intimately beneath him, drenched in moonlight and asking for pleasure, Merri reached over to set her bedside alarm. Her thigh accidentally bumped his in the process and frissons of heat coursed through her. "I can handle it." She shifted farther away, toward her side of the mattress, warning herself to keep all physical contact to an absolute minimum.

Ignoring the quickening of her pulse, Merri added as calmly as possible, "But what I would like is for you to take care of the kids, so I don't have to wake them and take them down to the barn with me."

Ready to assist her in whatever way he could, Chase nodded. "No problem."

Mind on the list. Mind on the list! Merri swallowed again. "Also, if your friends are up, maybe you could rustle up some coffee or juice or whatever till I get back to the house?"

He caught a strand of Merri's hair and tucked it behind her ear. "We can handle that," he promised, even more softly.

With her insides fluttering at the tenderness of his touch, she sucked in a breath. "And then, after that, I have to make those ten, crowd-size sweet potato casseroles."

He gave her a slow smile that suggested he would be a very patient, very thorough lover. The implication caused her to shiver all over.

His fingers stroked the inside of her wrist as she struggled to stabilize her soaring-out-of-control emotions. "I saw the recipe you laid out on the kitchen counter," he admitted.

Merri nodded, her breathing not nearly as deep or as even as she would have liked. "It was my mom's. She was famous for it. People asked for it every year." The only problem was, Merri thought worriedly, her rendition of the dish had never quite measured up to her mother's. No one said so, but she knew it. And after tomorrow, Chase would know it, too.

Misreading the reason behind her apprehension—the pressure of cooking for a very competitive, though appreciative, small-town crowd, Chase squeezed her hand again. "It's going to be all right."

Trying hard not to think about what it would feel like to kiss him again, privately this time, Merri nodded. She really had to stop wanting Chase like this. "I hope so."

Conversation lagged after that. Fatigue set in. Before Merri knew it, she had fallen asleep, only to wake five minutes before the alarm went off. Acutely aware of the big, warm man lying beside her, Merri turned her head slightly and opened her eyes. Damn, but Chase was gorgeous, even in his sleep. His profile was strong and even and so very male, given his high cheekbones, chiseled jaw and sensual lips.

He was lying on his back, as he had most of the night, head squarely on the pillow, with his arms folded behind it. Which gave her a great view of his muscular chest, nicely formed pecs and six-pack abs.

His forearms were covered with crisp hairs a shade darker than the short sandy locks on his head. Ditto his long, lean legs.

He hadn't touched her once through the night. Which was a shame, Merri decided, since she had very much wanted to touch him.

But he was right to stay on his side of the queen-size sleigh bed.

Although they'd agreed to make a baby together—when the time was right—it wasn't right yet. And wouldn't be until they got through the guardianship process. Until then, Merri thought, throwing back the covers, they had best err on the side of the caution.

So no more kissing Chase. No more tempting fate. No more anything except walking the straight and narrow.

THROUGH BARELY OPENED eyes, Chase watched Merri gather up her milking clothes—flannel shirt, down vest, jeans and boots. She slipped into the bathroom, and then a couple minutes later came out again.

Damn, but she was sexy, with her face scrubbed bare and her honey-blond hair swept up into an untidy knot on the back of her head. As sexy as she had been in those pajamas. He'd had an ache that wouldn't quit the entire night, which had made moving closer to her distinctly unwise.

His body might be telling him all systems were ready, but his head knew different. Merri wasn't the kind of woman who could handle sex with no strings, even for the purpose of making a baby they both yearned to have. She was the kind of woman who needed tenderness as well as passion. Love. Commitment.

And though he could easily give her three out of the four, his gut told him that she would never be happy unless she had the Real Deal feelings included in any bedroom alliance: love. Even if it was a mutually-agreed-on kind of caring.

So for now, he'd continue to feign sleep long enough for her to slip from the bedroom undeterred. Continue to wish they didn't have a million things in the way of the two of them getting close enough to make love, and hence get close enough to potentially be really truly happy together. But even though mind-blowing passion wasn't in their immediate future, he could still do what had to be done to give his new wife—and the inadvertent mother of his children—the domestic assistance she needed.

Once they were past the Thanksgiving holiday, and their company left, their lives would settle down quickly. A daily rhythm would be established. And with it, hopefully, so would the closeness and sense of family they all wanted and needed to make their lives complete.

Chapter Five

When she slipped into the kitchen to make a quick cup of coffee, Merri found she wasn't the only one up. Addie was already sitting at the table, dressed, restless and ready to go.

"Trouble sleeping?" Merri asked sympathetically.

She dipped her head in acknowledgment. "Guess I slept too much on the flight home. Going out to take care of your herd?"

Reminded that Addie had grown up on a farm in Minnesota, she nodded. There was something about living the rural life that created a near instantaneous bond in people. "Yep...that's right."

"Want some help?"

Merri knew it would go a lot faster if she did have assistance. And given how much she had to do before they all headed to the community center for the annual Thanksgiving dinner... "That would be great, thank you." She went into the mudroom, got out two pairs of Wellington boots, and handed a set to Addie. "Have you ever milked a cow?"

"I've done it the old-fashioned way—by hand."

Smiling, Merri went to the cupboard and pulled out an extra barn coat and work gloves. "We're a little more modern than that."

"Well, I'd love to see the operation. That is, if you don't mind me tagging along?"

It was easy to tell why Chase was so fond of Addie. Merri handed the other woman an insulated coffee mug. "I'd welcome the company."

As they drove out to the barns in the pickup truck, Merri filled Addie in on the specifics of the dairy operation. "Female calves are raised for two years before they produce milk, and milking is done twice a day—morning and late afternoon. Slim handles it most of the time, during the week, and I pick up a couple of shifts on weekends, when it's easier for me to get a sitter over to take care of the kids. Although I often take them to the barn with me, too."

Merri parked and got out of the truck.

As always, the herd was stabled in the adjacent barn at night, so it was easy to move them into the milking barn through the backing gates, and into the parlor. Addie helped Merri situate all twenty-four cows in their berths. Together they put out the feed and went up and down the aisles, sanitizing teats and hooking them up to the automated milking systems.

As they moved along, working nicely in tandem, Merri got the feeling that Addie was trying to work up the courage to talk to her about something. Merri hoped it wasn't more questions about how she and Chase had met.

Once everything was set, the two women stepped out to drink their coffee in the brisk November air, and admire the streaks of pink spreading across the horizon.

Finally, Addie spoke what was on her mind. Her cheeks a self-conscious pink, she blurted, "Don't worry about Starr when it comes to Chase."

Merri stiffened in alarm. Starr? The striking brunette who obviously had a big-time crush on Chase....

Addie lifted a hand. "It's obvious to everyone that she wants him to be a lot more than just her friend. She was hoping—since he's now out of the service—that she'd be able to make a play for him."

Merri ignored the sudden clenching of her abdomen. The idea that she and Chase had to prove themselves in family court, to Judge Roy, was stressful enough. Now she had to worry about someone trying to steal Chase from her?

She pulled in a breath and attempted to quell the sudden rise of anxiety within her. "You're telling me she hasn't made a move on him before?"

Addie shook her head soberly. "Starr knew she would crash and burn if she tried. Chase is a by-the-rules kind of guy. Fraternization within a unit is severely discouraged. Causes too many soap-opera-type problems, you know."

"So if you were to have a romance with a fellow soldier… one of you would have to be transferred out?"

"And Chase knows that and believes it's the right policy," Addie agreed. "It's why he never dated anyone within the unit, even on the sly. Plus, he was heartbroken by his previous fiancée."

Although Merri had been privy to that last bit of news, she'd never actually heard Chase's side of the story—just that he had fallen in love during his last years of medical school, and that the engagement was abruptly called off before he entered the military. True to form, he'd been tight-lipped about it ever since.

"Anyway, it's why we all came out here with Starr," Addie continued quietly. "'Cause we knew she was going to make a fool of herself over him. And we were hoping to sort of run interference—to keep things from getting too uncomfortable for either of them. Because at the end of the day, we think they both will still want to be friends."

Merri studied Addie's worried expression. "So you're telling me you think he's not interested in Starr that way."

She hesitated a second too long. "Well, obviously not, because he married you, didn't he?"

Yes. He had. For reasons Merri wasn't about to explain.

But would Chase have still married her if he'd known Starr was about to come after him, uninhibited by any military regulations that may have once stood in their path? Or would he have tried to solve the daddy dilemma another way in order to keep his options open?

Unfortunately, there was no way to know for sure.

No way she could ask Addie any of this.

"You all are so close," Merri said, instead.

"Crisis bonding." Addie walked through the wet grass and leaned against the pasture fence, her back to the beautiful Texas sunrise. She looked around, enjoying the sweet serenity of the morning. "Being thrown together in a field hospital forges quick, strong bonds. And it's not just on the battlefield where this occurs. It happens to people in any kind of crisis situation."

Like mine and Chase's, Merri thought, keeping an eye on the milking operation, and finding all was still well. She paced away from the open doors. "So the lot of you will be friends for life."

Addie's expression grew uncertain. "As long as we're in the military together, we will be." Briefly, pain flashed in her eyes. "But once a person is back in civilian life, and the high-stakes camaraderie that keeps a unit together no longer exists, well…" She shrugged and looked Merri in the eye. "In those situations, friendships sometimes fade or disappear altogether, because the closeness wasn't based on anything enduring.…"

Taking Addie's words to heart, Merri thought about the hospital grief group that had proved so important to her—in the months after her mother's death, as well as in the aftermath of her sister and brother-in-law's tragic accident. Both times, the support group had been a lifeline. But then, as everyone gradually healed and resumed their normal lives, the acute intensity of those friendships had faded.

They were all still friendly, of course. But not the way they had been while deep in mourning.

Merri swallowed. "Has the loss of this kind of friendship happened to you?" And more important, she thought nervously, would it happen to her and Chase? Not that they were all that close yet.

Addie nodded. "A few times, with people who have left our unit. But I'm still close to some individuals who left the army, too. So it depends."

Merri turned back to the fence, watching as the pale yellow sun edged over the sagebrush that dotted the far horizon. "What do you predict will happen with Starr and Chase?"

Addie finished the rest of her coffee, and replaced the lid on the stainless-steel travel mug. "To date, they are just friends. Although, Starr's always believed where there's a will, there's a way."

And Starr clearly had a huge crush on Chase. Merri's stomach twisted with anxiety. "So what are you trying to tell me? That she might make a play for Chase while you all are here?"

Addie's expression sobered. "If she does, it isn't anything you should be mad at Chase about. Because he's married to you now, and he's an honorable guy. The kind who always does what's right in the end."

Like throw away his freedom to marry me, to give the kids the best possible life. Merri sighed.

It took another two hours to finish the milking, check the production information on the computer, turn the cows out to pasture and clean and disinfect the barns with high-pressure hoses.

By the time they got back to the ranch house it was nearly nine. Merri was in desperate need of a shower and shampoo. Aside from taking care of their company, she still had the casseroles to make. Or did she?

The aromatic smell of brown sugar and sweet potatoes hit her the moment she walked in the door. Was it possible Chase had been cooking? she wondered in shock.

She slipped off her boots in the mudroom and walked into the kitchen, Addie tagging along behind her. There, standing in front of the stove, wearing Merri's favorite Williams-Sonoma apron, was a satin-pajama-and-slipper-clad Starr. Ovenproof gloves on her hands, she was lifting out four large casseroles. Four more sat, the picture of perfection, already baked. The last two were ready to be slid in to cook.

"Surprise!" Starr said.

"Look, Mommy!" Jessalyn called, from her perch on the counter next to Nissa and Davita. "Miss Starr cooked your sweet 'tatoes!"

Jeffrey nodded solemnly, clearly impressed. He beamed at Harmony and Polly, who'd been seated at the kitchen table, playing blocks with him, then pointed to the tattered piece of yellowed paper on the counter. "Just like the recipe said."

Addie looked as shocked as Merri felt, but not surprised. Clearly, Merri thought, this was stage one of Capture Chase's Heart. Complete with one button too many undone on Starr's satin pajama top.

"Wow," Addie said. She walked over to give a nicely dressed and showered Chase a friendly punch in the forearm. "You have been busy, soldier."

Merri nodded. Unable to vanquish the notion that she

had just been upstaged in her own home, she forced a perfect hostess smile. "Wow is right. Thank you all so much! I hope you got breakfast…."

"Oh, yeah. Chase fixed us his famous eggs and tortillas."

"He makes a mean cup of joe, too."

"We saved some for both of you, though."

"Thanks." Ignoring the unprecedented jealousy roiling in her gut, Merri forced another smile. "But I'm going to head for the shower. In the meantime, carry on."

"Do you think she's mad?" she heard Starr say behind her departing back. "Chase, honey, I think she might be mad. Why would she be mad…?"

Why indeed, Merri fumed, heading for the stairs. A scant two minutes later, she was stepping into the shower. Only to discover the fifty-gallon tank had been drained of hot water. What was left was at best lukewarm. Deciding, what the heck, maybe a cold shower was what she needed right now, anyway, Merri turned off the hot spigot and stood under the freezing spray.

By the time she had finished a quick lather and rinse of her hair and body, her teeth were chattering and she was shaking from head to foot. But her temper had cooled. Until a knock sounded on the door and Chase said, "Merri, I need to talk to you."

CHASE KNEW HE WAS IN TROUBLE the moment Merri stepped out of the bathroom, wrapped in a thick terry-cloth robe. She smelled of lavender, but her lips were devoid of their usual luscious pink color.

Upon closer inspection, he saw the goose bumps on her fair skin…and the way she was shivering. "Did you take a cold shower?"

New color flooded her cheeks as she ran a towel over her

hair, systematically blotting the dampness from it. "I didn't really have a choice. We're out of hot water."

He winced. "Sorry. All the gals were taking showers. Starr's headed there now."

"I hope she likes her water icy."

Okay, that had sounded very unhostesslike, which was in turn very unlike Merri. Aware that she had every right to be annoyed and stressed out, Chase took responsibility, too. "It's my fault. I had no idea we were short in that regard. I probably drained half the tank myself."

Merri regrouped and then flashed him a brief, purposeful smile. "I should have warned everyone." She shook her head, as if chastising herself for not thinking about it in advance. "When the old water heater went out last fall, I tried to conserve energy, and replaced it with a smaller model. With just the three of us here, we didn't need an eighty-gallon tank."

Chase leaned against the bureau, hands braced on either side of him, wondering what if anything she had on under that robe. Panties? A bra? Nothing at all?

He had to struggle to stay with the conversation. "If conservation is the goal, a heat-on-demand unit would be even better."

Merri tossed him a considering look over her slender shoulder, before starting to untangle her hair with a wide-toothed comb. "I considered it, but those models are a lot more expensive to purchase and install." She walked into the closet, hips swaying as she moved. "Right now I'm putting every penny I can spare into the expansion of the dairy, so it was out of my price range. At least for the moment…"

With his eyes on her sexy-as-hell legs, Chase followed her into the narrow space between the racks, speaking in a low, confidential tone. "It doesn't have to be, Merri." He watched as she searched through her wardrobe. The neckline of her robe gaped slightly, answering his earlier question. No bra, anyway. Just the soft, delicious curve of one plump breast.

He cleared his throat. "Now that we're married, I can help with things like that."

She kept her head averted, and focused on her mission—selecting the right thing to wear to the community event. As she held out a particular sweater, her teeth raked across her velvety soft lower lip. "I don't think we're going to run out of hot water very often. Unless you plan to have this many guests underfoot on a regular basis."

"You are ticked off that they're all here."

She grabbed a skirt, too, and a pair of matching suede heels, and then brushed past him. "On the contrary. I'm enjoying their company, as are the kids. And Addie was a great help with the milking this morning."

Chase watched Merri hang her outfit on the hook on the bathroom door. "Let's not forget that Starr pitched in to make all those sweet potato casseroles for the Thanksgiving buffet. Saving you a heck of a lot of time and work."

Merri returned to her dresser, pulled out a bra and panties and hose. "She certainly did."

Was that sarcasm underlying her low tone? Chase edged nearer. "I've heard of women being territorial about their kitchens…"

"Um-hmm." Lingerie in one hand, Merri pulled a pendant and earrings from her jewelry box. "Well, I'm not one of them."

But she certainly looked territorial about *something*.

"Mommy!" Jeffrey and Jessalyn burst into the bedroom. "That lady, the one in the apron, is screaming in the bathroom!"

Screeching was more like it, Chase thought, listening to the indignant, high-pitched sounds.

"Guess Starr just found out we're out of hot water," Merri said wryly. She made shooing motions toward the hallway. "Now if you'll excuse me, everyone, I've really got to get dressed and dry my hair."

"Kids," Chase murmured with outspread hands, ready to herd them downstairs. Once again, Jeffrey and Jessalyn looked at him as if he were persona non grata, and then fled in the opposite direction. Merri displayed the same intolerant attitude, which made it unanimous.

He was not yet an accepted member of this family, and at this rate, might not be for a very long while.

CHASE RODE WITH MERRI AND the two kids in her SUV. Addie and Starr took his pickup truck, while the other four women went in the van they had rented, all of them parking side by side in the community center lot. Chase opened the door for the twins, only to have them scoot over to the driver's side and wait for Merri to help them both out.

Give them time, he thought. *Closeness will happen.* He just had to remember not to push.

He shut the door and sauntered around to Merri.

He had never seen her looking prettier.

She had on a white cashmere sweater, a flowing, brown brushed-velvet skirt and suede heels. A silver pendant and matching earrings completed her holiday garb. "How are we going to do this?"

Jessalyn and Jeffrey tugged on Merri's hands, clearly wanting her to carry them.

"Honey, you're too big, you know that," she told Jeffrey. "You, too, Jessalyn."

No kidding. Chase thought. They were a good thirty-five pounds each.

Jeffrey argued, "You carry us sometimes."

"In emergencies," Merri allowed pleasantly, holding both

their hands and walking around to open up the back of her SUV. "Like when you get really scared or have a boo-boo."

Jessalyn gripped Merri's skirt before she could reach for the foil-covered casseroles. "We're scared now, Mommy."

"Yep," Jeffrey angled in close. "We really really are."

No, they weren't, Chase thought. They were testing her, a fact Merri seemed to know very well. He could hardly blame the twins, though, for trying to figure out where the boundaries were. They'd had some pretty big changes happen in their lives in the past week. Changes no one had prepared them for.

The kids had a right to be ticked off.

Starr sauntered forward and laid a hand on Chase's arm, with Addie right beside her. The brunette smiled up at him, the look in her eyes reminding him that she had been a pediatric nurse before enlisting in the military to care for wounded soldiers.

Chase gave her an encouraging nod.

Starr knelt down at eye level with the twins. "I can carry you, Jessalyn," she offered, with open arms.

Addie hunkered down, too. "And I can carry you, Jeffrey."

The twins beamed in acquiescence.

"That is, if it's okay with Merri," Chase interjected, remembering that though he was technically their daddy now, when it came to the kids and the ranch, Merri was still the one in charge.

"Sure." She admonished the twins with a look. "As long as you behave."

"We will," they promised in unison.

Starr and Addie picked up the twins.

Merri turned back to the sweet potato casseroles. There were ten large pans and five adults. "I think we should all carry one at a time and then come back."

"I can carry two," Chase offered, figuring that would save at least one return trip.

She shook her head. "These pans are disposable. They really should be carried by the bottom rather than the sides."

Because this was her show, he acquiesced. A minute later, all of them had a casserole in hand, and the people started toward the community center, with Merri taking the lead.

Other people were moving toward the door, too. Including Liz Cartwright and her family, the Briscoes, and Judge Roy with her husband and four teenage daughters. The latter group was loaded down with gallon jugs of iced tea and lemonade. They reached the door well ahead of the others and stepped inside.

Tables that would seat hundreds of local residents were festooned with cornucopia centerpieces and covered with tablecloths in beautiful fall colors. A sumptuous-looking buffet was being set up. People were bustling to and fro and calling out cheery hellos.

Merri turned to Chase as they crossed the threshold into the banquet hall. Unfortunately, he turned to her at the exact same time.

Their casserole dishes collided. Chase kept a grip on his, but Merri was not so lucky. In her effort to keep from dropping it altogether, she wedged it against her chest. The foil covering slipped at the same time that the flimsy aluminum pan holding it bent into a V. And a big glob of the perfectly prepared confection squished out onto her sweater.

Around them, everyone gasped, Merri included. Chase steadied his own casserole with one arm and gallantly reached out to steady hers, in a gesture that was too little, too late. The slippery contents oozed over top of Merri's hands, causing her to lose her precarious grip.

Chase swore in frustration as the whole casserole fell to the tiled floor.

MERRI DIDN'T KNOW WHAT WAS worse, the wetness seeping into her beautiful white cashmere sweater, the ruined food all over the floor or the bright orange streaks splattered across her skirt and Chase's slacks. He set his dish down safely on a nearby table while a collective gasp sounded.

"Mommy, you're a mess!" Jessalyne declared. She turned and pointed at Chase. "So are you!"

"Yeah. A great big one!" Jeffrey concurred, aghast.

Thanks. Merri grimaced and lifted a reassuring hand. "I know, kiddos, but we'll clean it up." Her face flaming with embarrassment, she knelt to recover the crumpled aluminum container. Chase knelt at the same time.

They bumped heads.

"Ouch!" they said in unison.

Merri didn't know whether to laugh or cry, so she did a little of both while Starr took charge with laudable military efficiency. "Let's get the remaining casseroles to the buffet." The nurse picked up Chase's dish and marched off, clearly not willing to risk any more of her culinary effort than they'd already lost.

Several mothers from the preschool appeared, their own children in tow. They shot Merri understanding, empathetic glances. "We'll take charge of the twins while you deal with this," they promised.

"Thank you," Merri said.

Addie jumped into the fray. "I'll see if I can get paper towels and cleaner."

Another guest bent to whisper in Merri's ear. "It can be hard to get in sync physically with a new husband. Don't worry, dear. It will come in time." The elderly woman patted Merri's shoulder.

Would it? she wondered.

What would Judge Roy think? There was barely a hint of reaction on her face as she and her perfect family glanced their way from across the banquet hall. But as Merri looked down in horror at the icky, sticky mess, she could feel the other woman's disapproval. This was such a disaster!

Chase gripped her hand and helped her to her feet. "I don't suppose you have any clean clothes in the SUV."

"No." Merri sighed. "And if I drive all the way out to the ranch to get some—"

"You'll miss the dinner," Chase guessed.

She nodded, her mood no longer anything close to thankful.

"Looks like it's your lucky day." Merri's friend, Emily, suddenly appeared, waving a key in her hand. "Just so happens that Dylan and I have extra clothes at the Daybreak Café. They're in my office upstairs, behind the party room. And there's a bathroom, too. So—" she gestured to Merri and Chase "—help yourselves to whatever fits."

"I'm sorry," Merri apologized, still feeling hideously embarrassed as the two of them walked away.

"I ran into you," Chase said sheepishly.

"We ran into each other," Merri corrected in exasperation.

He shrugged and wrapped an arm about her shoulders. "Doesn't matter," he teased. "The end result is the same. We're both a big mess!" He gestured expansively. "Jeffrey and Jessalyn said so."

Not sure whether his response was for show or comfort, Merri leaned into him. "Do not make me laugh. This is so not funny."

His lips crooked up at one corner. "Tell me about it," he

grumbled in return. "Do you know how long I spent picking out this ensemble?"

He had looked very handsome, Merri thought. Too gorgeous for his own good. Seeing him in a jacket and tie reminded her of their wedding day.

They walked past the closed sign and opened the door to the shuttered café. The empty restaurant was a peaceful oasis after the bustling community center.

Acutely aware of him, Merri led the way up the stairs, to Emily's private office. The closet in the corner was filled with clothes. Outfits for riding, for casual dinners in town, and fancy affairs. Merri began sorting through them.

Chase plucked up a sequined black dress with a plunging neckline. "This is nice," he quipped.

"Yeah. Like I'm going to show up in *that*."

His eyes gleamed as if he was imagining it.

Merri flushed. "You could wear a tuxedo."

Chase stepped into the bathroom and studied his reflection in the mirror. "Actually, I think I can get most of this out with a little water."

Merri eyed the stains on his pants, which started just below his crotch and fanned out in tiny splatters from the thigh down. "Lucky you."

He reached for a washcloth and dampened it beneath the spigot. While he dabbed at the spots on his dove-gray shirt, then began working on the charcoal fabric of his trousers, Merri continued rummaging through the options. Finally, she emerged with an ivory silk tank, a black wool skirt and a long cranberry cardigan. "Hopefully, these will fit. Although my shoes aren't going to match at all." She lifted a trim ankle, showing off her brown suede pump.

Chase regarded her leg with mock solemnity. "Now, that's a crime."

Grinning, Merri aimed a fist at his sternum. "Cut it out."

Amber eyes lighting with mischief, he caught her forearm and held her hand over his thudding heart. "You cut it out."

Merri caught her breath at the intent in his gaze. "Chase..."

The next thing she knew his head was lowering, tilting slightly to one side. And then his lips were on hers.

Chapter Six

Heaven help her, the man could kiss. And he wasn't just any man; he was her husband. If only the marriage was based on the kind of abiding love a couple should have for each other, Merri thought. But it wasn't. And she had to keep reminding herself of that. Otherwise, she'd think that the way he was kissing her and holding her was proof that he was falling in love with her.

And that couldn't be true.

They had a deal. This was a marriage made to support a family. To enable them to do best by the twins, and add another child to the mix. A child she would carry.

Meanwhile, he was pressed against her, deliciously warm and hard, his lips moving tenderly over hers. Desire swirled through her, making her pulse race, and turning up a fierce, thudding heat in the feminine heart of her.

The kiss was meant to curb frustration and restore humor to a situation that was fast getting out of control. At least that was what Chase had told himself when he ignored Merri's gasp of pleasure and took her into his arms.

But that was before she had slayed him with that look—the one that invited him to do what no one else had been able to accomplish—to try and tear down the barriers surrounding her heart, to find the soft vulnerable woman she tried so hard to shield from further hurt.

And, Chase thought with a rush of overwhelming want and need, damned if he wasn't determined to do just that.

Their lips meshed, more perfectly still. He plunged his tongue into her mouth, kissed the corners, realized she was kissing him back with a passionate resolve that wrenched a low groan from his throat.

Tightening his grip, he hauled her all the way against him and shifted her so her back was to the wall, the only sounds the rasp of their breathing and the low murmur of delight when he slid his hands beneath the hem of her cashmere sweater and cupped her breasts with his palms.

Her nipples pearled, and he slipped a thumb beneath the satin bra, basking in the feminine feel of her.

She leaned into his touch, her fingers finding their way beneath his shirt, the waistband of his slacks.

Wanting. Just as he wanted.

And that was when they heard it. The sound of footsteps coming up the stairs to the second floor of the café. A feminine voice calling out, "Chase! Merri? Are you up here?"

Chase and Merri broke apart, disheveled, and out of breath, right before Starr rounded the corner.

Chase's friend took one look at them and emotion flickered in her eyes, then disappeared.

"We were talking," he said.

Something less pleasant flickered across Starr's face. "I can see that," she said, her glance moving over his shirt, then Merri's sweater, and the proof that resided there.

MERRI FOLLOWED STARR's glance. Chase's shirt had barely been soiled before. Now, sweet potato casserole was smeared across the entire front of it. The creamy orange goop and flecks of chopped pecan were even more deeply embedded in the white cashmere.

Plus his shirttail was hanging out of the front of his pants.

While Chase seemed to have recovered from their passionate interlude, Merri was one guilty and embarrassed wreck.

"I'm sorry if I interrupted anything," Starr continued pleasantly with a poker face. "I just wanted to make sure everything was okay. And it occurred to me, Chase, that you probably had some clothes at the hospital, in your locker there, since you often go straight from office hours into surgery. I was going to offer to go and get them…"

Merri looked at Chase. Realized, to her further humiliation, that he had already thought about that, and had instead chosen to come here with her. To make sure she was okay, or use the opportunity to put the moves on her?

Not certain how she felt about consummating their marriage by indulging in some clandestine pre-Thanksgiving feast nooky on the sly, Merri drew a deep breath and said, "That's a really good idea, Starr. Actually, you can both go together."

Chase lifted a brow, obviously realizing she was trying to get rid of him, pronto. Merri lifted a palm before further protest could be made, and directed them to the door. "I'm fine here. Honestly. And dinner is set to start in another twenty minutes, so we all better get moving."

Once they departed, Merri took advantage of the privacy to pull herself together and deal with the fact that she had almost surrendered all her standards and had sex with Chase, then and there. Hadn't she told herself when she ended her last relationship that she would not let herself be used again or treated as less than she was? She deserved respect. So did Chase.

More important still, she wanted to harness her emotions and be in control of the situation. She wanted to act while thinking clearly, not while in the throes of uncontrollable lust. Because at the end of the day, there was no confusing lust with love.

"YOU WANT TO TELL ME WHAT'S going on?" Liz asked Merri, a scant fifteen minutes later.

Breathless, and still glowing inwardly from having been thoroughly kissed, Merri scanned the room for the twins, saw them already seated at the table reserved for their age group. With relief, she noted the kids looked very happy as they colored their kiddie place mats.

She spotted Emily, too, all the way across the room. Merri plucked at her borrowed clothing and mouthed a thank-you.

Emily smiled and waved back, mouthing *You're welcome.*

Aware that the attorney was still waiting for an explanation, Merri turned to Liz. "What do you mean, going on?" she asked, stalling for time while she tried to figure out just how much to reveal.

"You and Chase and the twins walk in with six of Chase's woman friends."

"Oh. That." Merri waved her concern away. "They're good friends. Medical personnel from the army unit Chase was in."

Liz eyed the group of attractive young women with an assessing gaze. "And they're all staying with you. While you're essentially still on your honeymoon."

Merri was acutely aware it had only been four days since the wedding. Four very eventful days. "It's a long story. But yes…Chase and I invited them."

"The twins seem to like them."

"As do I."

Liz considered that. "Where's Chase?"

To Merri's dismay, he chose that moment to walk into the community center, with Starr by his side, acting for all the world as if she, not Merri, were his wife.

Liz frowned as her glance cut to the Roys. The judge was eyeing Chase and Starr, too, and the attorney sighed. "This does not look good."

Tell me about it.

Frowning, Liz continued her summation with lawyerly calm. "First, you and Chase are about as uncoordinated and out of sync as any couple I have ever seen, bumping into each other and getting food all over both of you. Next, the two of you take off to change clothes, only to come back alone, looking…" She paused and shook her head. "And then fifteen minutes later, he shows up with that incredibly attractive shamelessly smitten brunette."

Her pulse racing, Merri lifted a palm. "I can explain."

Liz lifted a hand, too. "I don't need to hear it. I don't *want* to hear it. Just be aware that Judge Roy is privy to all this, too."

Their attorney had a point. "So what do you suggest I do?" Merri asked nervously.

"Demonstrate to everyone that what the two of you are proposing to the court is in the best interest of the twins. That there is every reason to put faith in you as a couple— and a family."

CHASE DIDN'T KNOW WHAT had gotten into Merri or Starr. All he knew was that he was sandwiched between them, and both were acting as if he were the most fantastic man on earth. Smiling at him, engaging him and each other in conversation, constantly touching his arms.

Addie kept trying to intervene, too, and divert all the attention to her, in a way that was unusual, to say the least.

While Nissa, Davita, Harmony and Polly enjoyed their meal and looked on in bemusement.

Not that the twins were about to come in last, either. Jeffrey and Jessalyn sat nestled together on the other side of Merri. Demanding that she—and only she—cut their turkey, and take the offending green beans and sweet potato casserole off their plates.

Meanwhile, everyone they knew stopped by their table on the way to and from the buffet table to congratulate Merri and Chase on their new marriage. And each time it happened, she tensed.

Chase knew how she felt. Because it did seem a little insincere.

And that, he knew, was going to have to be rectified.

They couldn't go back into Judge Roy's court, swearing they were "family," when right now, anyway, they were anything but that.

Maybe making love would help. That, and him finding a way to get close enough to the twins to become the daddy they needed and deserved....

"Earth to Chase. Earth to Chase," Starr teased, touching his arm again.

What was with all the physical possessiveness? He turned to his former coworker, wondering how he could get her to back off without hurting her feelings or making a scene. To his left, he heard Merri push back her chair.

"Hurrah! We get to go play!" the twins shouted exuberantly, running off to the temporary children's center set up in one corner of the banquet hall. Looking flustered, Merri rushed to catch up with them.

Starr kept right on talking, raving about the hospitality of his home county, but Chase only had eyes for the woman he had married.

Damn, but Merri was gorgeous, even in borrowed clothes and shoes that didn't match.

Smiling, she settled the kids with the teenagers supervising the indoor play area, then turned and plunged back into the crowd of friends and neighbors, to his surprise making made a beeline for every single, cute, thirty-something man there. One by one, she patted them on the biceps, whispered in their ear and urged them to tag along with her.

Within ten minutes, she had half a dozen guys surrounding her and was walking back to the table where Chase and his lady friends sat, enjoying their after-dinner coffees.

An unfamiliar pang of jealousy knotted Chase's gut. Was this some sort of payback for the onslaught of women around him?

Merri gestured magnanimously as they reached the table. "What we have here, fellas, are six ladies in need of the blue-ribbon tour of Laramie, Texas."

The men grinned, exchanging glances with each other as well as their feminine quarry. "I think we can handle that," one drawled.

"Particularly if all you ladies want to stay around for the band that's going to play later this evening, over at the dance hall."

"I don't know…." Starr demurred. "I'm not sure we should desert Chase or Merri, since we're all leaving tomorrow…."

He stood and nudged her gently, "You should go. It'll be fun. Besides…" He turned to his wife. "Merri and I will be busy with the kids this evening. 'Cause I don't think there's any way they're going to last that long."

Acting all wifely again, Merri confirmed, "They won't."

Starr wrinkled her nose. "You're really going to miss all the fun?"

Chase wrapped his arm around Merri's shoulders and

gave her a playful buss on the temple. "Not all the fun." He winked salaciously and everyone laughed.

"Well," Addie murmured, looking straight at Starr, "they *are* newlyweds!"

NEWLYWEDS INDEED, MERRI thought with a silent snort.

She didn't feel like Chase's wife. And he certainly wasn't acting like a husband to her, except that he was annoying her right now, the way she had seen almost every husband annoy his wife at one time or another. Unfortunately, for everyone's sake, Merri knew she had to follow their attorney's advice and demonstrate that she and Chase were a viable couple who would do right by their children.

"Can I have a word with you, hon?" Chase asked. "Privately?"

Not if it meant they would end up kissing again, here of all places. Merri gave him a look only he could see. "Can it wait? I've got to talk to Paige and Kurt...."

"Actually—" Chase began, tenderly tightening his grip and pulling her closer to his side.

At that precise moment, the hospital chaplain passed by, beaming. He gave Merri a thumbs-up. "Best sweet potato casserole I've ever eaten, bar none."

It figured, Merri thought drily, the way her day was going....

"Don't know what you did to it, but the chaplain's right—it is fantastic," Deputy Rio Vasquez agreed enthusiastically as he passed by about the same time, another serving of casserole in hand. "Your mother's recipe never tasted so good in all the years you've been cooking it."

This would be the one time she would get wildly enthusiastic compliments.

"So good," a cowboy chimed in, "that it's now completely gone." He looked at Merri wistfully. "You did your mama proud."

"Thanks." Honor dictated that Merri give credit where it was due, no matter how embarrassed she felt. "But I didn't make it this year." Smiling self-consciously, she pointed at the stunning nurse on the other side of the room. "Starr did."

The men fell silent as they realized they had just put their foot in it.

"But I'll let her know you guys all really liked it," Merri promised, before turning to Chase. "In the meantime, I've got to let the twins know they're going to go home with Kurt and Paige and the triplets for a play date, while I tend to the herd back at the ranch and do the milking."

A mixture of surprise and hurt flashed across Chase's face. "I could have watched the kids," he said quietly. Realizing this was a private discussion, their companions drifted away.

Guiltily, Merri realized that she hadn't even thought to ask him if he wanted to do so. She was going to have to work on this co-parenting thing. "This is sort of our tradition," Merri explained, with an apologetic glance. "But if you want to go with them to Paige and Kurt's home, I'm sure it would be okay with them," she finished kindly.

Another wave of tension ran between them, as if he, too, knew how out of sync they were. Ready to do what he could to remedy that, he looked her in the eye. "How about I help you instead?"

Chase? Operating a milking machine? Cleaning out the barn? Merri shook her head. "Thanks, but Addie already offered to assist me again."

Chase aimed a thumb over his shoulder, his lips lifting in a grin. "Addie looks like she has her hands full with that cowboy."

Well, what do you know? Merri thought, watching Addie flirting shyly with her gentlemen companions. Good for her!

Merri turned back to Chase, still not able to see him assisting her. Like it or not, he belonged in a hospital, with a bevy of adoring assistants around him. She wrinkled her nose. "It's a dirty job."

He fixed her with a deadpan look. "I can get dirty."

Heaven help her, she was reading all sorts of things into that remark. Shrugging, Merri ignored the shimmer of sexual attraction between them. "Suit yourself."

Realizing he had gotten to her, upping the ante another notch, he chuckled. "Thanks, hon, I will."

She let her gaze rove over his tall, solidly built frame and powerful shoulders. "And stop calling me hon." When he came closer, she could feel his body heat. "Okay, sweetheart."

She put her hands on her hips and returned his smoldering gaze. "I don't like that endearment, either, cowboy."

He rubbed his jaw in a thoughtful manner, eyeing her thoughtfully. His gaze took her in, head to toe. "Babe?"

Her smile widened as the flirtatious mood between them deepened. "What do you think, hunk of burning love?"

He rocked back on his heels and squinted speculatively. "Sugar?"

Merri stifled her amusement and drew an indignant breath. "Doesn't really fit, either, honey bunch."

Chase laughed, the sound deep and flirtatious. Awareness sifted through her as he shifted the fall of her hair away from her face and leaned forward to whisper in her ear, "Well, it's not going to be darling."

The warmth of his breath warmed her skin. Refusing to think about hauling him into her arms and kissing him again, she retorted, "Wise decision, hubby dear."

"Well, then—" He wrapped a possessive arm about her

waist and gave her a decisive look meant to needle her even more. "Wifey it is, then."

Merri groaned at the thought, even as she let him guide her toward the door.

The facetious argument about what sort of endearments they could use for each other carried them all the way out to the ranch. Given the seriousness of the problems facing them—both in court and on the home front, it was a relief to talk about something utterly nonsensical. "Maybe I should just call you sheik," Merri decided, when they finally parked in front of the ranch house.

Chase got out of the SUV, glad they were finally going to have some time alone together. Their first real solitude since the afternoon they had decided to marry.

Grinning, he fell into step beside her. "Sheik?"

Merri paused to unlock the front door, then swept inside in a drift of lavender perfume. "You've already vetoed stud and honey, baby cakes and sweetie pie."

Merri carried their stained clothing into the laundry room and deposited it in a wicker basket marked Dry Cleaning. Whirling again, she slid past him and headed for the staircase.

Lazily, Chase followed. "But sheik?"

Inside their bedroom, Merri grabbed a clean set of work clothes and disappeared into the master bath. "Kinds of fits with the 'harem,' don't you think?" she said, around the mostly closed door.

Chase began to strip down, too. "So you *are* jealous."

"I am not." Merri emerged, borrowed set of clothing in hand.

Chase admired the way she looked in her flannel shirt and faded, threadbare jeans. He strode to the closet and rummaged for his jeans. "I was," he admitted as he pulled out a thermal, long-sleeved T-shirt, too.

"Of what?" Merri sat down to pull on a pair of wool socks.

"You." Chase closed his fly. Tugged the shirt on over his head. "With all those guys you rounded up."

Merri slanted him a skeptical glance as he sat down next to her on the bed.

He shrugged, thinking about the way he'd felt when he'd seen her flirting with them. "I didn't know what you had in mind."

Her green eyes glimmering, Merri scoffed. "A seven-some?" She slapped her hand on his jean-clad thigh and bounded right back to her feet. "Seriously, Chase!"

He stood, too, locking eyes with her. "Well, okay, not that, but…" His mood turned deeply serious again as he admitted, "I think of you as mine."

He watched for her reaction.

To his frustration, she looked more wary than ever. "To a point," she said slowly, "I am."

He hooked his arms about her waist and pulled her close. "More than just a point," he said, wanting more than ever to take things to the next step.

Merri saw the desire in Chase's eyes. She splayed her hands across his chest and hitched in a bolstering breath. "Chase…" She moaned as his lips blazed a fiery path across her forehead, dipping down to the sensitive spot behind her ear.

"We're never going to feel married unless we behave like we're married," he coaxed, working his way down the slope of her throat.

Merri arched against him. Her fingers clutched his shirt, even as she struggled against the sensations coursing through her body. She closed her eyes, thinking maybe it wouldn't feel so erotic, so right, being here with him this way, if she couldn't see him.

"This isn't the way," she protested weakly.

He slid a hand beneath her chin and lifted her lips to his. "Tell me that in five minutes," he murmured, "and I'll believe you."

The next thing she knew they were kissing. Hotly. Tenderly. Merri shifted her hands to the nape of his neck and curled her fingers into his hair. Unable to help herself—the truth was she wanted to claim him, too—she surged against him, loving the taste and touch and wonder of him. He was everything she had ever wished for, and she could feel his arousal, pressing hard against her, summoning up her own blossoming need. She wanted him desperately and she let him know it with a sweet, searing kiss in return.

Chase knew it was medieval of him, but he wanted to put his stamp of possession on Merri. He wanted her with him, with absolutely nothing held back. Anchoring his arm around her waist, he guided her toward the bed. *Their* bed. Fell onto it with her, so she was beneath him. Her body was throbbing everywhere his was.

"Okay... You're convincing me," she gasped, slipping her palms beneath the hem of his shirt, running them across his skin. "But we've got chores to do, and kids to pick up later, so we have to make this fast."

Chase knew what she was thinking. As long as they kept this purely physical and matter-of-fact, their hearts would stay intact. He reached for the buttons on her shirt, uncovering her a few inches at a time. The swell of her breasts peeked out from the lace of her bra. He undid the clasp, revealing creamy skin and pink nipples. His lips followed where his eyes had gone. "Not too fast."

But again, she wanted to keep things casual, with all the caution their situation required, and none of the heart.

Knowing that wouldn't work in the long run, not for her, Chase kissed her to remind her of what they could have, given half a chance. He kissed her to show her what he wanted them to have, in the end. He kissed her out of frustration for the way everything was evolving, and the way that it wasn't.

And she kissed him back, responding to his passion, meeting his need. Until he knew that what was happening had less to do with their marriage than the way she made him feel, as if he had to be part of her life, and she his. Not just for now…so they'd be more in sync as a married couple. But because there was something here. Something real and vital and worth exploring. Something they couldn't ignore.

He had no more time to contemplate that, however, because she surged against him, tugging and unzipping. "I can't wait…."

Needing, wanting her—and the closeness she offered— he tugged and unzipped, too, and it was like Christmas Day as they wiggled out of the rest of their clothes and climbed onto the bed. Their naked bodies pressed up against each other in the fading afternoon sunlight streaming through the blinds and he stroked her dewy softness. "Here?"

She yielded to him with the sure sense of a woman. "Yes. Oh…yes…there!" Arms wrapped around him, she kissed him again, trembling, clinging to him. He kissed her back, until she surrendered to him completely, the sweet whimpering sounds in her throat a counterpoint to the lower, fierce sounds in his.

"And here?" Chase asked, drifting lower, ready to take each moment as it came.

She caught his head in her hands. "Oh, yeah."

He parted her knees and his own pulse pounding, stroked the insides of her thighs. She arched to receive him, bringing him closer yet. "So. Very. Nice."

And then words deserted her as he made his next move, delved even deeper, and Merri came apart in his hands. Loving the way she looked at him then, as if he was her hero and she was his princess in waiting, he couldn't resist teasing, "Beginning to see my point?"

Her dreamy smile widened.

She wanted to keep things simple.

Yet he knew they were going to get complex.

Mischief sparkled in her green eyes. "As long as you see mine." Smiling sassily, Merri shifted and took control, her silky hair sliding over his chest. Downward she glided, wrapping her hand around him, using the same gentle rhythm he had used on her. Suddenly, he was the one on the edge. Her lips found him, loving him slowly and thoroughly. Chase groaned, desperate to have her. "Now I'm the one who can't wait."

She laughed, and the sound of her pleasure unleashed him. He shifted so Merri was beneath him. Filled with the exquisite need that drove them both, he held her hands above her head, then kissed her again, long and hot, wet and deep, until he was pretty sure neither of them could have given their own name, and it felt so damn good their breath was rasping and their hearts were pounding. Until there was no doubt about what was coming next. "Tell me you want this," he commanded. *Tell me you want me.*

She gasped and bucked, near bursting. "You know I do."

A shudder racked him and then ran through her, as well. He entered her with one smooth stroke, lifting her, holding her close. Willing to play it her way for now, he murmured, "Tell me this is just the beginning."

Her eyes locked on his. She surged against him obediently and kissed him, unable to hold back. "It's just the beginning."

Her sweet compliance sent him further toward the edge.

Satisfaction roared through him, perfect and all-encompassing. He moaned, and ground his hips against hers, touching his thumb to where they were joined. She murmured his name, pleading softly. He answered her by going even deeper. Sensation built upon sensation and the world fell away. Together, they spiraled into ecstasy and beyond.

Chapter Seven

As soon as Merri caught her breath, the doubts starting
creeping in. What had she done, except very possibly make
the baby she wanted so much, with a husband she knew did
not love her and probably never would? At least not in the
way she had always wanted. Panicked, she began to ease
from his embrace.

Chase tightened his hold on her. Pressed a kiss into her
hair. And looked at her with his what-I-could-do-to-you-
if-I-only-had-the-chance-to-make-love-to-you-again eyes.
"Where are you going?"

That quickly, she found herself at the melting point. "The
barns."

To her dismay, he saw right through her pragmatic reply.
"No rest for the weary, hmm?" he murmured, calling her a
liar with everything he didn't say.

Merri bit her lip. "You knew we had to do the milking
when we stopped to…" She faltered, unsure what words
to use.

His eyes tracked the sheet she held to her breasts. "Make
love?"

Despite the fact they weren't in love with each other, that
was what it had felt like. Merri nodded shyly.

Chase caught her wrist and pulled her back into bed. His
amber eyes glimmering with suppressed devilry, he focused

with laser accuracy on her mouth. "How could five minutes of cuddling be so wrong?"

Trying not to imagine what it would feel like to throw caution to the wind and have him buried deep inside her one more time, she stated as casually as she could, "I didn't think you were the type."

He shrugged. "I'm not," he told her. "At least in the past I haven't been."

"Then it's probably best we not change that," Merri retorted.

"Why not?" He stroked a hand down her back.

Resisting the urge to curl into the inviting hardness of his chest, she eased away for the second time. Caution was what she needed here. What they both needed. "I don't want us to be confused."

He lifted an eyebrow, a silent question.

"We may be married but we're hardly friends," she explained.

Those laugh lines appeared again at the corners of his eyes. "Getting to know each other better in the biblical sense might help speed things up."

Merri tossed her head. "Trust me, Chase. Events are going fast enough as it is."

His gaze turned compassionate. "Too fast?"

And then some, Merri thought. His understanding attitude prompted her to admit, "I swore when I ended my relationship with Pierce that I wouldn't allow myself to indulge in any more whimsical thinking."

Chase studied her face, waiting for her to go on.

She sighed and perched on the edge of the bed, fingering the sheet tucked around her breasts. "When I moved in with Pierce, I knew he wasn't ready for marriage. He told me he wasn't going to be for a couple more years."

"But you got engaged nevertheless," Chase recalled.

Merri rose and began collecting her clothes, piece by piece. "He did that to meet me halfway."

Reluctantly, Chase rose and began to dress, too. "Only...?"

She tugged on her panties, then her jeans. "I'm pretty sure Pierce knew then that he was never going to want to get married to anyone. It just wasn't his thing." Quickly, she slipped on her bra, too. "But I couldn't accept that. I wanted it all back then. I wanted to have a husband and a family and the home that I had never had, growing up with a single mom. And I was sure if I was patient and loving and kind enough that I would eventually get what I wanted." She let out a wistful breath. "Allowing myself to hope that way almost destroyed me."

Chase sobered. "I get that you were hurt, but the two situations aren't the same. I want the same things you do. I've always wanted them."

Merri watched him zip up his fly. "Did you also want to be loved?"

Chase went still. He kept his eyes locked with hers for a long minute. Finally, he said, "I assumed that would be the case if I ever got there."

Merri stepped closer, guessing, "But it wasn't a necessary part of the equation."

He braced his hands on his hips, his eyes guarded now. "No."

Merri looked down, her fingers trembling slightly as she buttoned her flannel shirt. "It always was for me."

"Past tense," Chase observed.

"Fate and circumstances have conspired to make me lower my expectations."

He sat down to put on his boots. "Which is why you agreed to marry me, without love," he speculated.

She went to the bureau, picked up her brush and ran it through her hair. "I wanted to be fair to you, protect the kids—and give them a complete family, plus have another child."

Chase frowned, walking over to stand beside her. "That's all pretty cut-and-dried."

Slowly, Merri set her hairbrush down on the dresser and turned to face him. "If we're going to be successful, Chase, it has to be."

"So no cuddling."

She tilted her chin, affirming flatly, "No cuddling."

Because cuddling with Chase could tempt her to fall in love with him. Merri did not want to love another man who—in the end—did not love her in return.

"MAYBE WE SHOULD STAY A few more days," Starr said the next morning. The gorgeous brunette looked at Chase from her place at the table, eager to be of assistance in any way she could.

Which would have been fine, Chase thought as he spooned coffee grounds into a filter, had it not been for her obvious crush on him. A crush that had seemed to be well under control—until his former coworker arrived in Texas, anyway.

"It seems like you-all are swamped," Starr continued, rising and carrying her plate to the dishwasher.

Chase put another pot of coffee on to brew, then moved to the breakfast room windows overlooking the play set in the backyard. Yesterday had been a great day, sunny, cool, crisp. Today, the typical November gloom was back. The temperature was hovering just above freezing, and rain was threatening.

"I don't have to be at work until eight this evening," Chase said. He had pulled nighttime duty at the E.R. the rest of the weekend, so he'd be sleeping at the hospital tonight.

Merri had been up at the crack of dawn. She had refused his help with the milking, going out with Addie instead, while he entertained their houseguests and watched the twins. As much as Jessalyn and Jeffrey would let him, anyway, given they preferred just about anyone to him.

Merri walked downstairs now, fresh from the shower.

Her hair still damp, she was wearing a pine-green corduroy shirt, denim jeans and boots. She helped herself to the breakfast casserole she had prepared the night before.

"You-all don't worry about that." Lounging against the counter, Merri forked up a bite. "I just have to do the milking this evening, and I've got a babysitter to help me with the kids during their dinner and bath. Slim will be back to take over the dairy operation tomorrow morning."

"We have a lot more people to see," Harmony pointed out.

Davita nodded. "My mother is expecting us in Shreveport tonight."

"And my folks want us in Nashville by Monday," Polly added.

"We don't want to let anyone down," Nissa interjected.

Chase provided further encouragement. "You-all should enjoy your road trip, as planned, before you split up to spend Christmas with your families."

Outvoted, Starr went to collect her suitcase.

Merri, Chase and the twins walked the women out. Watched as they loaded everything in their rented van. Hugs and goodbyes were exchanged all around and the kids waved enthusiastically until the servicewomen's vehicle left the drive and disappeared down the county road. Together, the four of them walked back into the house.

Chase barely had a chance to savor the sense of family before the twins pulled away. "Can we get our blocks out?"

"As long as you pick up your mess when you're done," Merri agreed.

"Hurrah!" They ran off to the play area in the sunroom.

"What next?" Chase asked.

Merri picked up the folded linens on the sofas and carried them to the laundry room, alongside the kitchen. She set them down next to the washing machine, glanced at her watch and sighed. Although they had just finished breakfast, the morning was nearly gone. "I'm not sure. I've got a lot to do…"

The overwhelmed expression on her face was all the invitation he needed. "What's most urgent?"

"The grocery store." Merri sorted clothes. "I really need to go. But I also have a lot to do here, and who knows how much I'll actually get done if the twins decide not to cooperate."

He moved back to give her room to work. "Then why not let me go, and take the kids with me?"

Merri poured detergent over the towels, shut the lid and turned the washer on. "I don't know if you've noticed, Chase, but the twins haven't exactly warmed to you."

He winced. Talk about hitting him where it hurt. "Exactly. Which is why we need to spend more time together, pronto."

Merri leaned against the dryer, arms folded in front of her. "Forced proximity?"

"It's been known to work. Besides, it will be fun."

Merri rolled her eyes and pushed past him in a drift of lavender perfume. "You wouldn't say that if you had ever taken them to the market."

Chase followed her into the kitchen. "Let me do this, Merri," he said quietly. "It's a first step toward becoming a family."

She stared at him a moment, then finally relented. "Okay," she said, waving a lecturing finger at him. "But don't say I didn't warn you."

AN HOUR LATER, CHASE was pulling into the grocery store parking lot, twins in tow. "I don't see why we had to go with you," Jeffrey grumbled.

"Yeah," Jessalyn said. "I wanted to stay with Mommy."

Chase put the list in his shirt pocket, then got out to assist the children. "You'll get to be with Mommy later. Right now she needs us to buy some groceries."

Jeffrey crossed his arms in front of him, making it difficult for Chase to get the safety harness off. "We don't want to share Mommy with you anymore," he said with a glare.

Well, at least I know what the problem is, Chase thought.

"Yeah," Jessalyn added, with equal seriousness. "Can you go home now? We decided we don't want you to be our daddy, after all."

Trying to hide his hurt feelings, Chase cast a look at the increasingly gray clouds overhead. Was it too much to hope that the rain would hold off till later? "We are going home as soon as we get the stuff."

"Not our house. *Your* house. We want you to go to your house," Jeffrey retorted.

"The Broken Arrow Ranch is my home now," Chase explained patiently.

Jeffrey scowled. "No, it's not. It's ours."

Jessalyn nodded in solidarity, then told Chase sternly, "You need to go away now."

Chase exhaled. Talk about running the gauntlet...

Figuring this discussion could wait until later, he took a calming breath and suggested mildly, "How about we do this? How about we all try cooperating for a change?"

Silence fell. The twins' expressions remained recalcitrant. And Chase knew for a fact how stubborn they could be.

When all else failed, there was always the carrot and the

stick. It had worked on him when he was a kid. Heck, it still worked, when the stakes were high enough.

He straightened and rested one arm on top of the SUV door. Casually, he announced, "There are cookies in it for anyone who is a big help to me in the store."

He knew they were hungry. They'd barely touched their breakfast or the peanut butter and jelly sandwiches Merri had insisted on making for them before they left the ranch.

Aware the children had finally stopped arguing with him, he upped the ante. "Any kind of cookies you want. You get to pick."

The ice in their demeanor thawed. Slightly mollified, the twins relaxed enough to allow him to unbuckle the straps and get them out of their safety seats, and out of Merri's SUV.

Chase held their hands as they entered the store. Merri had warned him not to let them roam free. He pointed to a shopping cart shaped like a car, with two side-by-side child seats, each sporting its own play steering wheel. "How about we ride in that?"

The twins readily agreed. Chase lifted them in and fastened their belts, and they were off. "You're not pushing very good," Jessalyn pointed out.

That was because the big, clunky thing was twice the size of the other shopping carts, nearly as wide as the aisles and had no turning radius to speak of. "I'm still getting the hang of it," Chase said.

He stopped in front of the Free Cookie display at the front of the store and got out one sugar cookie for each of them.

"I want two," Jeffrey announced.

"One each," Chase reminded the twins.

In search of the first few items on his list, he hit the produce aisle. It was crowded with other shoppers, most of them women. Everyone, it seemed, wanted to stop and congratulate him on his new job, and on moving back to the ranch with his beautiful now bride and those precious children.

The twins had finished their cookies. They were getting restless.

"Thanks so much. I've really got to go." Chase pushed on without the zucchini Merri had asked for. But the broccoli was handy, so he got that instead.

On to the meat aisle.

He scanned the packages, did not see top round, so bought sirloin steak.

"I'm still hungry!" Jeffrey said loudly.

"Yeah, I want another cookie, too!" Jessalyn announced.

"When we get home," Chase promised, rounding the corner as best he could, into the dairy and juice aisle.

There, in front of him, was Judge Roy. Like everyone else, she was dressed in jeans, shirt and a waterproof jacket, probably because the courts were closed for the Thanksgiving holiday. Beside her were two of her teenage daughters. The girls seemed perfectly behaved as they helped their mom get what was on her list.

Recalling what the judge had said about not trying to pull anything over on her, Chase nodded briefly in recognition, then hurriedly pushed on, catching a corner of the doughnut display in the center of the aisle. Several boxes tumbled to the floor.

Embarrassed, he bent to get them.

"I want those!" Jessalyn shouted.

Don't let them talk you into getting too much sugar, Merri had warned. *They'll want everything sweet that they see.*

"I think we'll just stick to cookies."

The twins opened their mouths to protest.

Aware of Judge Roy behind him, Chase leaned forward and promised very very quietly, "Remember? Be good, and you get to pick whatever kind of cookies you like."

As always, they drove a hard bargain. "Both of us?"

"Yes," Chase said, deciding it was only fair. "One kind of cookie for each of you."

"Hurrah!" The twins cheered so loudly every shopper in the aisle turned to look at them and smile.

Unfortunately, Chase couldn't find the next few items on the list.

The bread rack was ridiculously empty. There was every kind of jelly but grape. The kids were ornery and restless.

"I'm tired!" Jeffrey shouted.

"I'm hungry!" Jessalyn proclaimed, even louder.

Chase grabbed strawberry jam and headed down the cookie aisle.

With the judge in the store, the sooner he got out of there the better.

Jeffrey pointed to the extra-dark mocha biscotti. "I want those ones, up there."

Coffee flavored? Chase shook his head. "I don't think you're going to like them, buddy."

"I will, too!" Outraged, Jeffrey put a hand on the steering wheel and stood up in the cart.

When and how had he gotten his seat belt off? Chase wondered.

"And I want those." Jessalyn pointed to soft oatmeal raisin.

Anchoring one hand around Jeffrey's waist to steady the little boy so he wouldn't fall, Chase reached over to get the cookies his sister wanted, and dropped them in the cart. "Good choice."

"Now mine!" Jeffrey demanded.

Again, Chase refused. "Pick something else. Something that Mommy likes for you to have."

Wiggling out of Chase's light, easy grasp, Jeffrey folded

his arms in front of him. "You said it could be my choice," he pouted.

Oh, great, was that Judge Roy coming down to the cookie aisle, too? Chase got hold of Jeffrey once again, anchoring him with one arm around his son's waist. "It can be, but…" Chase had to use his other hand to move the cart slightly to the right, so Judge Roy and her daughters could get by. Unfortunately, the wheels were stuck and the big cart wasn't budging. Chase set Jeffrey back in his seat so he could use both hands to maneuver the cart.

"Thanks," the judge said, pushing past.

"Then—" Jeffrey bounded out of his seat and jumped up onto the steering wheel on his side of the cart "—I'll get it myself." He lurched forward, losing his balance in the process. Chase caught him, but could do nothing about the half-dozen packages of cookies that were knocked down.

They clattered as they hit the floor. Judge Roy and her daughters swiveled to look, as did everyone else within earshot. Just that quickly, total chaos reigned.

"You broke my cookies!" Jeffrey wailed, and let out a sob of distress that echoed throughout the store.

MERRI HAD JUST WALKED through the automatic doors of the grocery store when she heard a familiar sob that, once started, seemed to go on and on and on.

Picking up speed, she rounded the corner of the cookie aisle, so quickly she nearly mowed down the customers trying to get away from the piercing cries.

"Judge Roy!"

The woman nodded, her expression courtroom bland. "Seems like your son needs you."

"Mommy!" Jeffrey wailed. "Make Daddy go away!"

"Yeah, we don't like him!" Jessalyn sniffled between sobs.

It was a disaster. "Okay, you two," Merri soothed, gathering them into her arms. "Hush now. Hush."

The twins clung to her and their tears subsided.

Chase stood next to her, wearing that look of suppressed hurt and quiet disappointment she was beginning to know so well. A feeling that she was pretty sure he hadn't had much experience dealing with until now.

"I'm sorry," Merri said. "I knew this was a bad idea."

"Which is why you're here."

"I got to thinking, right after you left, that they're just too tired from all the activity of the past few days to handle any kind of shopping. So I got in the ranch pickup truck and drove here." Just in case.

Chase shot her a grateful look. "I'm glad you did." He rubbed the tense muscles at the back of his neck, admitting ruefully, "I could use the help. I've hardly gotten anything on the list."

"It's not a problem." Merri reached over and squeezed his arm. "We'll work together and wrap this up in no time."

An hour later, they were back at the ranch. Merri let the twins sit at the kitchen table and eat cookies and drink milk while she and Chase put the groceries away. When they'd finished, the children were led to the living room, where they settled on the sofa with their blankets and stuffed animals, and watched their favorite Thomas the Train movie.

Ten minutes into it, both were sound asleep. Merri switched the DVD off and returned to the kitchen, where Chase stood, breaking down some cardboard for the recyling bin.

"How do you do it?" he asked her, clearly discouraged. "It's like you have a magic touch."

Merri smiled wanly, her heart going out to him. "Not always."

He peered at her, sizing her up. "Most of the time."

She squeezed his hand. "You've got to stop trying so hard."

He caught her wrist before she could disengage. "Or in other words, I need to back off."

Merri nodded. "It's going to happen," she promised softly. "They will accept you as their father. But only when they're ready."

The two adults fell into a thoughtful silence. "And when will that be?" he asked eventually.

"I'm not sure." Merri moved closer. "You have to have faith."

His mouth took on a rueful twist and he rubbed a hand across the shadow of beard on his jaw. "I thought you didn't believe in wishful thinking."

"There's nothing magical about them needing a father." She turned to face him, squeezing his hand again. "Believe me, they are acutely aware they haven't had a daddy. They will love you, in time."

Chase anchored an arm about her waist and pulled her close. "You're sure?"

"Very," Merri said. She could see the desire in his eyes, feel the heat in his body. Why pretend this wasn't happening when it was? In the past four and a half years, she had rarely thought about herself, and never done anything to tend to her own needs and desires. Being married to Chase made her want to change all that. He made her want to experience life—and pleasure—to the absolute fullest. Gazing up at him, she rose on tiptoe and wound her arms around his back. He threaded his hand through her hair, then fastened his lips on hers in a riveting kiss that stole her breath and weakened her knees. The hardness of his chest pressed against her breasts. Lower still, she could feel the proof of his desire. She arched against him, wanting, needing so much more. Yet knowing they weren't alone, this wasn't for show, and with the two children sleeping just a room away...

Merri splayed her hands across his chest, flummoxed by her reaction to him. "Chase."

She'd told herself she was going to wait. Get her feelings and fairy-tale fantasies under control again, before she pushed desire to the limit.

Reluctantly, he drew back. "I know. They might wake up."

That wasn't why she needed them to stop, but if he wanted to think it was...

It was better than telling him she was worried she might fall in love with him. Worried that her love would again not be returned.... Not in the same deeply romantic and passionate way, anyway....

Knowing this arrangement would work only if the playing field was level, and determined to do what was right and honorable for both of them, Merri marshaled her defenses.

She thought about the evening ahead, and the fact that she would be able to go to bed at a decent hour—albeit alone—while he was at the hospital, on duty. Her heart went out to him once more. "Do you want to take a nap, too, since you have to work all night?" she asked with concern.

The look he gave her said he would rather sleep with her. Now. Probably naked. Although it wasn't "resting" he had on his mind.

Yet as always, he was motivated by doing the right thing, for all of them. Frustration turned to acceptance. "Wake me in an hour?" he asked gruffly.

Merri nodded. "Sure thing." Then she watched, her heart breaking a little, as he walked off.

Chapter Eight

Merri held the phone to her ear. "I understand," she said quietly, so as not to wake the still-napping twins.

Pacing to the window, she gazed at the ever deepening gray of the late-afternoon sky. "These things happen," she soothed. "You go rescue your brother before the storm hits. I'll take care of things here. Yes…give everyone in your family my best."

Lamenting the fact that yet again her life had just gotten more challenging than it needed to be, Merri headed up the stairs.

She walked down the hall toward the guest room.

Chase wasn't there.

She kept going to the master suite and found him fast asleep, sprawled out on top of her bed. Shirt unbuttoned, hands folded behind his head, he was the picture of sexy masculinity. And Merri felt her heart give a little jolt.

Why did he have to be so darn attractive? And why couldn't she stop thinking about how it had felt to make love with him?

More to the point, why was he in here instead of the guest room? Did this mean he intended to sleep with her from now on, even though their visitors had left?

Having him beside her all night would definitely make it easier to make love. It would also help them feel married, and would leave her more emotionally vulnerable. But maybe, Merri thought, given their very complicated circumstances, there was no way around that.

Maybe, she told herself sternly, she just needed to take things one day, one moment, at a time. And right now she had a task to complete.

Aware this was something a wife would do for her husband, Merri approached Chase and sat on the edge of the bed, touching the side of his face gently. "Oh, sheik?" she teased, doing her best to keep her tone light, playful. Unemotional.

Sleepy amber eyes opened. He sandwiched her hand between his palm and the roughness of his beard. "Hey." He flashed her that slow, sexy smile she loved so much, kissed the inside of her wrist. Another thrill went through her. Merri cleared her throat. "It's been an hour. Actually, a little over…"

Chase rubbed his eyes, then pushed himself up on his elbows. His expression ready-to-head-to-work sober, he listened intently, then asked, "Twins still asleep?"

Merri grinned at how much he already sounded like a doting dad. Seeing an opening to lighten the tension with a joke, she replied, "It's extremely quiet." She leaned closer, waggling her brows and inadvertently getting a whiff of his masculine scent. "So what do you think?"

Affection lit his gaze. "That they're still snoozing away."

Merri grinned back. "Correctamundo! You win the prize."

Chase sat all the way up and stretched his upper body. "Babysitter here yet?"

Merri tried not to notice how the smooth cotton fabric of his white T-shirt, visible beneath his shirt, molded to all that sinew. What the man could do for an underwear ad, should he ever be asked…

She pushed her desire aside long enough to answer his question. "Sadly, Amy, the babysitter, is not coming. Her younger brother was in a fender bender in San Angelo. Bobby just got his license a few months ago. He's freaking out. Neither of them have been able to get hold of her folks, and Amy isn't sure his truck is all that drivable, so she's going to rescue him."

Chase sat up against the headboard, his thigh nudging hers in the process. "I take it he wasn't hurt?"

Merri noticed Chase didn't move away. Nor did she.

Aware of the body-to-body heat, even through their jeans, she swallowed. "Not a scratch, luckily. Apparently his truck is another matter. Bobby drove up on the curb, so the axle may have some damage."

Chase groaned in sympathy. "That's an expensive repair."

"No kidding." Merri thought about how intimate it was, sitting here like this, just talking, sharing their day. Who would have thought this part of marriage would be so comforting and fun?

"Anyway," she continued, casting a glance at the late-afternoon gloom outside the windows, "I hate to ask…but it's going to start raining any minute, and I've got to bring the herd in and do the milking."

He looked at her with none of the frustration he'd experienced earlier still evident. "You want me to watch the kids?"

She had to hand it to the man, he was resolved to be successful at whatever he did. And that went double in the daddy department. "Would you mind terribly? You said you didn't have to leave until eight, and I can wrap things up in around two hours."

He waved off her concern. "It's not a problem."

Merri stood, to let him up. She propped her hands on her hips. "You say that now," she warned, not purely in jest. "They weren't exactly cooperative earlier, and they're going to be even crankier when they wake up, because they're so off schedule." Which meant he'd have his work cut out for him.

Chase got to his feet in one smooth motion. "I wouldn't worry about it. They can't loathe me more than they already do." He paused humorously. "Can they?"

When she just looked at him, Chase ambled closer, towering over her. "I'm joking, Merri." He cupped her shoulders and the warmth of his touch was almost as soothing as the tenderness of his grip. "Of course I'll watch over them," he stated, searching her eyes. "I'm their dad. It's part of my job. Unless—" he narrowed his gaze "—you'd prefer I care for the herd instead?"

"No. It'll go a lot faster if I do it."

Chase picked up his boots and sat down to tug them on. "Are the Christmas decorations still kept in the attic?"

Reminded that he had once lived here, too, Merri nodded. "Same place as always." There were some things about the Armstrong ranch that never changed.

He stood and headed for the door. "What about my stuff? Is it still in the attic, too?"

Merri followed him into the hall, where she reverted to her the-kids-are-still-snoozing whisper. "You mean the belongings you left at the ranch when you went off to college?"

He nodded, his handsome face filled with purpose.

Curious as to what he was up to now, Merri smiled. "No one's touched the boxes since you put them there."

He looked surprised but pleased. "Can you give me ten minutes before you head out, to find what I need?"

It was fun being on his team, Merri decided. "Sure."

"Thanks." He patted her arm, more as a friend would than a husband, and headed off. Seconds later, she heard him milling around on the third floor.

Merri grabbed warm clothes. By the time she had her

long underwear on under her jeans and shirt, he was tromping back down the stairs, several storage boxes in his arms.

She wrapped a washable cashmere scarf around her neck. "Want to tell me what this is all about?"

He grinned, as masculine and supremely determined as ever. "I'd rather surprise you."

CHASE SAW MERRI OFF, then went into the living room, where the kids were still asleep. He set the boxes on the floor and opened them. A wave of nostalgia hit him as he lifted the first Lionel train car out of the box. Chase hadn't seen any of this in years.

Not since his dad had died, and he had considered himself too grown-up to mess with toys. They'd been in the attic ever since.

No more.

He lifted out one piece after another. Tracks, engines, control box, cord. Then he heard the stirring behind him.

Recalling Merri's advice not to push, he kept his back to the kids while carefully dusting off each and every piece. There was a telltale thud as four small feet hit the wood floor in perfect unison and scooted closer.

One shadow fell to his right, the other his left.

The small, sleepy-eyed figures came even closer, dragging their blankets and stuffed animals in their wake.

"Where did you get that train?" Jeffrey finally asked from Chase's left.

Trying not to feel too encouraged, he responded casually, "It's mine. My mom and dad gave it to me for Christmas one year, when I was a kid. It's been in the attic."

Jessalyn came closer, too, flanking him on his right. "Does it have a name?"

Belatedly, Chase realized all the cars and engines in the Thomas the Train video the twins had watched before drifting off to sleep had names. He looked at the gold leaf lettering on the side of the black engine. "The train's name is Lionel."

Jessalyn pointed to a coal car. "What about this one?"

Chase read the identifying script decorating that one, too. "That's Pennsylvania."

Chase plugged the train in, hit the lever that would send it forward on the track. The train had juice; he could hear the engine going. Unfortunately, the wheels weren't turning. He switched it off.

The kids edged closer. "Is it broken?"

"Just a little rusty." Chase picked up the four cars he'd put on the track. "Let's see what we can do to make it work."

He headed for the kitchen.

As he had hoped, the kids trailed along after him.

"Whatcha doing?" Jessalyn asked curiously, climbing up onto a stool at the counter.

Chase rummaged around for some WD-40. Coming up empty, he reached for a bottle of cooking oil and plucked a basting brush out of the rack. "I'm going to try and oil the mechanisms on this thing."

Jessalyn wrinkled her brow in warning. "That's for cooking."

Desperate times called for desperate measures. "You're right—it is," Chase replied, appreciating her effort to keep him out of the doghouse with Merri. "But I think it will work on the train, as well."

"Cool," Jeffrey said.

Keenly aware that he had a captive audience, Chase got to work, carefully adding a little canola oil to all the moving parts.

When he had finished, he tried it out. Sure enough, the wheels and axels began to turn.

It was hard to know who was beaming more, him or the

twins. He picked up all the toys. "Ready to see if it will work?"

Jessalyn and Jeffrey nodded enthusiastically.

Together, the three of them returned to the living room, where track pieces were spread out in the middle of the floor.

Chase went back to assembling them. By the time he had finished hooking everything up, the twins were as involved as he had hoped. "Okay," he said, on a wing and a prayer, "here goes."

He hit the switch. The train engine moved forward, smooth as silk. Jeffrey and Jessalyn's faces filled with wonder. Mesmerized, they cuddled even closer to him and watched the train go around, accepting him for the first time since he had come back to Texas.

MERRI LET HERSELF INTO THE ranch house, took off her boots and hung her rain slicker up to dry. Given how long she had been gone, she had half expected to hear crying or at least whining. Instead the place was amazingly quiet, except for…was that a *whistle?* And a *bell?* And her children—*their* children, she reminded herself sternly—laughing and talking excitedly?

Merri followed the sounds to the living room.

Her heart leaped at what she saw: Chase sitting on the floor in front of an old-fashioned electric train set, with a child on either side of him. Jessalyn had the bell and whistle. Jeffrey was manning the gear box.

"Okay, stop it," Chase said, "and reverse the train."

Jeffrey carefully did as ordered.

"Ring the bell!" Chase told Jessalyn.

She instantly complied.

Abruptly, the kids became aware of Merri. Their eyes shone with happiness. "Mommy, this is so much fun!"

"We get to play with Chase's trains."

"I see you all survived without me," Merri drawled.

Chase looked as content as she had felt the first time she'd held the children in her arms, as tiny babies. "We did." He smiled, obviously enjoying the simple domestic scene as much as she was.

Pleasure rushed through her. Was this what family life would eventually be like? Once adjustments were made? Still feeling a little chilled, she stepped closer to the hearth and stood with her back to the flames. "Want me to rustle up some dinner before you head off to the hospital?"

Chase shot her a grateful glance. "That'd be great," he said.

"We'll stay here and play, Mommy," Jeffrey said.

And they did. Right up until the moment they had to come to the table to eat. The only difficult part was afterward, when Chase had to leave for his shift. "But we don't want you to go," Jessalyn said, stamping her foot.

Jeffrey pouted. "Yeah, we like having you here!"

Chase hunkered down. "I'll be back tomorrow morning."

Since it was the weekend, there was no preschool. "You'll see him after breakfast," Merri promised.

The twins looked at him. For a moment, Merri thought they were going to launch themselves into his arms. Instead, they just smiled shyly and scampered away.

Merri turned to Chase. "Good work, champ."

He looked truly happy, hug or no hug. He reached for her, drawing her into his arms and bussing her cheek. "It's definitely a start."

"Mommy, you are not being fair!" Jeffrey said the next morning.

"Yeah," Jessalyn grumbled. "We want to play with Lionel and Pennsylvania!"

Merri glanced at the digital clock on the microwave. She had expected Chase home around eight-thirty. It was now nine, and there was no sign of him. "I told you before," she explained patiently. "The electric train belongs to Chase, and only he knows how to use it. So you're going to have to wait for him."

Jessalyn studied her suspiciously. "It's not that hard for grown-ups," she argued.

True, but Merri wasn't about to interrupt the fragile thread of cooperation and contentment that had sprung up between Chase and the twins over that heirloom toy.

She smiled again. "I'm sure Chase will let you play with the trains when he gets home from work. In the meantime, why don't we bake some Christmas cookies and surprise him?"

As expected, sugar was the magic potion that cut short all temper tantrums.

With the kids' help, Merri made the spritz dough and filled the cookie press. The kids took turns pushing the trigger that loaded them on the trays.

Merri turned the oven on to preheat, then handed the twins bottles of colored sprinkles.

Jessalyn decorated the miniature stars and Christmas trees on one tray, Jeffrey the other. When they were finished, Merri slid both trays into the oven to bake.

While they waited, Jessalyn propped her chin in her hands. "Mommy, is Chase really going to be our daddy now, and not just our uncle?"

Merri had an idea how confusing all this was for the kids. Trying to explain the complex adult reasons behind her marriage to Chase would have just made it more so. So she stuck to the facts, saying only, "He really is."

Silence fell as the twins exchanged looks. Finally, Jeffrey asked, "Is Chase going to be an army doc and go far away again?"

"No. I'm not," a deep reassuring voice said.

They all turned to see Chase walk into the room, several big shopping bags in hand. Joy flooded Merri as she savored the feeling of being there with him.

"What have you been up to?" she asked her new husband. On impulse, she stood on tiptoe and kissed him on the cheek.

Chase grinned. Wrapping an arm about her waist, he hauled her close and kissed her back, his lips briefly brushing her temple. He gave her waist another squeeze as he turned his attention back to the kids.

He set the shopping bags on the kitchen table. "I got to thinking last night that it's Christmastime, not just for us, but for Thomas the Train and all his friends."

When he started hitting the mark, he really hit it, Merri thought, impressed to see he wasn't wasting any time.

Jessalyn jumped up and down. "Like Percy and Rosie and Sodor?"

"Yes. So on the way home from work I stopped and got some stuff to help your trains celebrate, too."

The children's faces lit up with excitement. Chase shrugged out of his jacket. Still clad in surgical scrubs, he asked Merri, "Is it okay if we use the coffee table in the living room for now?"

"Go for it!" She beamed.

The timer dinged. Merri turned to take the cookies out of the oven, then joined the rest of the family.

"I didn't know if you'd ever had a Christmas village." Chase covered the table with a large rectangle of white felt. He pulled out four beautifully painted wooden pieces.

Merri admired the pharmacy, train station, grocery store and church. "We haven't. But it's a terrific idea."

Chase lifted miniature toy pine trees, lampposts and park benches from the bags. "Where do you think these should go?" he asked the kids.

While they were engrossed with the setup, Merri slipped from the room. She returned with a plastic storage bin of wooden train tracks and wooden trains and handed them over, then headed out again.

"You don't have to go," Chase called after her.

Not about to interrupt what this very special bonding between Chase and the kids, she called back, "Uh, yeah, I do, if we ever want to get the rest of those cookies baked!" There were approximately four dozen left to prepare.

Merri was just taking the last pan out of the oven when Jessalyn and Jeffrey came running in. "Mommy, come and see what we built! It's Christmas for our trains!" They took her hands, and she followed them into the living room. Chase was lounging on the floor next to the coffee table. A miniature village had been set up. He'd never looked more relaxed.

"It's beautiful," she said. "Did you say thank you?"

"Thank you!" the twins chorused shyly. They smiled at Chase broadly and sat down next to him to play.

Merri walked over. Golden-brown stubble rimmed his handsome jaw. He had circles of fatigue beneath his eyes. Reminded that he had been up nearly nonstop for almost twenty-eight hours, she said, "You doing okay?"

He shot a telling look at the kids, telegraphing his growing love for them. "Better than okay."

"Need breakfast?"

"I had something at the hospital cafeteria, about five."

"Need a bed?" Merri asked, beginning to get the hang of being his wife.

He exhaled. "Unfortunately, yes."

Merri continued to study him compassionately. "What time do you want me to wake you?"

"Four o'clock."

That was only five hours away. Merri wrinkled her nose. "Is that going to be enough rest?"

"Plenty. I want to have time to run another errand before I head back to the hospital this evening."

"Then four it is," she promised.

AS IT TURNED OUT, MERRI didn't have to wake Chase up. He came down at three-thirty, freshly showered and shaven. "You-all up for an errand in town?"

The twins, who had been too excited to nap, scowled uncooperatively. "We want to play trains," Jessalyn declared.

"This is something for Christmas, to help us continue to get in the spirit of the holiday," Chase qualified casually,

All play stopped. "Is it going to be fun?" Jeffrey finally asked.

Chase shrugged. "Are the trains fun?"

The twins nodded. "Lots of fun," they said in unison.

"Then I think you'll like this, too." He walked over to the coat tree to get their light jackets.

The rain from the previous day had cleared up, and it was bright and sunny outside, although still a bit nippy. He helped the children on with their coats, then gallantly handed Merri hers.

"What about me?" she teased, enjoying their newfound family togetherness. "Will I like this, too?"

"Hmm." Chase tilted his head, studying her with impish eyes. "I guess we're going to have to find out."

Minutes later, they were in Merri's SUV, driving to town. Chase was behind the wheel; Christmas music was playing on the radio. "How about a little hint?" Merri asked curiously.

"Uh…" He chuckled. "No."

"But we want to know!" the kids chorused.

"Okay. I'll give you a few clues. It's big. And prickly," Chase said.

"A dinosaur?" Merri asked, playing along.

"Mommy! A dinosaur won't fit in the car!"

"It will if it's a toy dinosaur," she argued.

"But it's not a toy," Chase said.

"Hmm." Merri tapped her fingers against her lips in a parody of thoughtfulness.

Jessalyn bounced up and down. "What color is it?"

"Green." Chase smiled. "It's green and big and prickly…."

"I know!" Jeffrey shouted.

Jessalyn yelled, too. "It's a Christmas tree!"

"You all are so smart, you figured it out." Chase tossed Merri a warm glance. "I thought we would pick one out together, since it's for all four of us."

"Can we decorate it together?" Jessalyn asked.

Merri nodded. "I think we'll have time."

They arrived at the Laramie Rotary Club lot. It was brimming with beautiful Afghan pines of all shapes and sizes. "So the question is," Chase drawled, as they roamed up and down the aisles, "do we want a Charlie Brown Christmas tree? One that is little and needs lots of love? Or do we want a middle-size one, that isn't too tall or too short? Or a great big tree that's taller even than me?"

The twins looked at each other. "I want a little tiny one that needs lots of love," Jessalyn said.

"I want a great big one that is bigger than Da—uh, Chase," Jeffrey said.

Merri caught her breath. Jeffrey had almost called him "Daddy."

But not quite. She saw a flash of mixed joy and wist-fulness in Chase's eyes. Again, her heart went out to him.

Chase went on cheerfully, "Okay. We have one vote for a tiny one, one vote for a big one. What does Mommy want?"

Merri propped her fists on her hips and played along. "Putting me on the spot here, aren't you, buddy?"

Chase spread his hands. "Everybody's got to vote."

"I noticed you haven't voted yet, Daddy." Merri deliberately used the moniker Chase coveted and deserved.

His eyes twinkled in response. "That's cause I'm waiting for you. Ladies first and all."

The children giggled. "Yeah. It's your turn, Mommy. You have to vote, too," Jeffrey told her.

"Then I want a medium-size one," Merri decreed.

"Your turn." The kids looked at Chase.

"I say…" he paused until he had them all waiting with bated breath "…there's only one way to break a three-way tie."

"THREE TREES," MERRI murmured when they had finished securing the evergreens onto the roof of her SUV.

Chase tipped the teenage helpers handsomely, then turned and pointed to the cargo area. "Don't forget the wreaths for the front and back doors."

Merri breathed in the fragrance of fresh-cut pine and man. He was so handsome and kind. "Don't you think it's a little excessive?"

"For our first Christmas together?" Chase murmured. "I think it's just right."

Merri warned, "You're going to spoil them."

"I'm going to spoil all of you." He took her chin in his hand and kissed her, right there in the parking lot.

A jolt of desire swept through her. Shocked but elated,

Merri rose up on tiptoe and kissed him back. If today was any indication, she thought happily, they were going to have a very Merry Christmas indeed.

Chapter Nine

"The current schedule must be killing you," Jackson Mc-Cabe said to Chase. "Working twelve-hour days, five days a week, and then some."

It was certainly wreaking havoc on the fragile bonds of his marriage, although as the new guy, he wasn't in any position to complain. Chase sat down opposite the silver-haired chief of surgery. "It's a lot easier than what I did in the military." There, he'd been on call literally twenty-four hours a day, seven days a week.

"Still, what works for the surgeons whose kids are grown and out of the nest probably doesn't work so well for you."

Over the past ten days, Chase *hadn't* been seeing as much of his family as he would have liked. "The day shift is okay. The twins get up at six most mornings, so I'm able to have breakfast with them before I have to leave for the hospital, at seven-thirty." In order to make the thirty-minute drive and arrive on time.

"And in the evenings?" Jackson pressed.

Chase did miss having dinner with them. "Merri's been trying to keep them up so I can see them when I get home at eight-thirty, and then tuck them in. Of course, when I've had the night shift, I'm home to have dinner with them and help with the bedtime routine *before* I head to work at the hospital."

"But you don't see them at all in the morning when you're on nights," the chief surgeon surmised.

Chase frowned. "Right, because they leave for preschool at eight-thirty. Although sometimes we pass each other on the highway."

He winced. "That must be hard."

It was, particularly when the twins were upset because he wasn't around enough to play trains with them.

"How is Merri adapting to the new schedule?" Jackson asked with the compassion of a long-married man.

That, Chase thought, was hard to tell. Outwardly, she was pleasant and cheerful and cooperative, every inch the supportive wife and doting mother. Inwardly, was another matter entirely.

Now that their company was gone, she had fixed up the guest room again and suggested he sleep in there, to ensure he got enough rest.

That wasn't what he wanted, but he understood. Merri got up at five most mornings, even when she wasn't doing the milking, so she could shower and dress and have some time to herself before the twins awakened. To ensure she got enough rest, she usually went to bed by nine-thirty or ten.

"It's hard, being married to a doctor." Jackson continued, "Especially when you're a newlywed."

"Merri's been a trooper. And she's busy with her own business, too," Chase stated.

"Still, I imagine she'd like to see a lot more of you. So the other surgeons and I were talking, and we're going to make some changes to our shifts, moving the time from six to six, instead of eight to eight."

"Thanks. I appreciate that."

Jackson grinned. "And to precipitate the change, we're sending you home early today."

It was barely two in the afternoon! "I'm only halfway through my shift."

"I'll cover for you. You just go home and enjoy that new wife and those kids of yours. Let 'em know how much they mean to you."

Gratitude welled within him. "I will," Chase said with a smile.

Figuring that as long as he was going to surprise Merri, he might as well bring home dinner, too, Chase changed out of his scrubs and stopped by the Daybreak Café. The restaurant, which served only breakfast and lunch, was closing. But Emily was there, along with her husband.

"Got anything I could just put in the oven for dinner tonight?" Chase asked.

She pointed to the specials listed on the blackboard. "King Ranch casserole, for the adults. Macaroni and cheese for the kids. Plus a couple of salads and some grilled vegetables?"

"Sounds great." Chase shared the twins' sweet tooth. "Dessert?"

"How about a fresh apple pie and some vanilla ice cream?" Emily winked. "Got to celebrate while you can, you know." She disappeared into the kitchen.

Huh? Chase looked at Dylan. "Any idea what your lovely wife was hinting at just now?"

Dylan scoffed. "C'mon, Chase. The whole town knows."

"Knows what?"

"That Merri was in the obstetrician's office this morning. One of the other pregnant ladies said that she had that special glow…." He paused. "You didn't know she had an appointment?"

"She probably wanted to surprise me." Was Merri pregnant? They'd kissed numerous times, but made love only that once, roughly two weeks before. So she couldn't be very far along, if she was in fact pregnant. Was that why she hadn't wanted to continue sleeping with him? Because she had sensed the deed was done and she had been successfully impregnated the first time out of the gate? Or was it simply because she was still trying to get used to being married to him, before they leaped into bed again? The only thing Chase knew for sure was that he didn't want to rush her, any more than he already had. Because Lord knew she deserved some kind of courtship and a get-to-know-each-other-better period.

"Hey." Dylan dragged him out of his fog. "We didn't mean to upset you. It is good news, isn't it?"

"If that's what the news is," Chase said.

Was that what he wanted? How did he really feel? Besides completely stunned—and once again, disappointed at being inadvertently shut out in the whole baby-making process.

"You are the daddy, right? I mean, tell me I didn't put my foot in my mouth—that you didn't marry Merri so suddenly because she found herself in a situation courtesy of someone else?"

Chase scowled at his friend. "Of course not. If Merri's pregnant, I'm definitely the father."

Emily walked back out, carrying two big bags of takeout. The stricken look on her face said she had heard enough to realize what was going on. "I'm sorry, Chase. We just figured that, being a doctor and her husband, you would know."

Was that why Jackson had given him the rest of the day off and gotten the other surgeons to adjust their schedules? Had the chief of surgery heard the latest on the rumor mill?

"Of course, it's none of our business if Merri is pregnant," Emily continued kindly. "We're sorry. We didn't mean to overstep."

Get a grip. Chase held up a hand. "It's okay. It's no secret that Merri and I are trying to, um, expand our family. So…" He shrugged and smiled. Maybe it was all happening sooner than they had ever imagined it could.

MERRI WAS SITTING IN THE kitchen, in front of her laptop computer, when, to her surprise Chase strode in, carrying two large bags from the Daybreak Café. He smiled at her and set the food inside the fridge, clearly a man on a mission. "Where are the kids?"

"At a play date." Battling a self-conscious flush, she pushed back her chair and stood. "What are you doing home?"

He closed the distance between them and wrapped his arms around her, as had become his habit when coming and going. "I got the afternoon off for good behavior."

Merri sank into the comforting warmth of his tall, strong body. He smelled and felt so good. "That's nice," she murmured against his chest.

"The chief of staff has also changed my hours to make them a little more family friendly."

Merri listened while Chase explained. She pulled in a stabilizing breath, then stepped back as casually as she could. "That's really nice."

"You look like you've been busy." He helped himself to a Christmas cookie from the trays cooling on the counter.

Merri swallowed. "I got a notice that a few of the gifts I ordered in early November are not going to be arriving before the twenty-fourth, after all, so I'm getting a few more things on the internet, for the kids, with overnight delivery."

He looked at her assessingly. "Anything else?"

"What do you mean?"

He held her gaze for a long time. "Maybe something you want to tell me?"

Merri tensed. "Like what?"

He caught her hand and reeled her in close. "Like the fact you were seen coming out of the obstetrician's office this morning."

Heat flooded Merri's face. Pressing a palm to his chest, she stepped back a pace. "How do you know that?"

He lounged against the counter and folded his arms. "People were talking about it at the café over lunch. Emily overheard and told Dylan. By then, the word was you were pregnant, so he congratulated me."

"Wow." Knees wobbling, Merri sat down on a kitchen stool. "Like a real-life version of the telephone game."

Chase lifted an eyebrow. "You're not answering the question."

"I wasn't aware there was a question," she protested weakly.

He came toward her, then stood with his hands braced on the counter edge on either side of her, lowering his face till they were nose-to-nose. "Are you pregnant?"

Merri hitched in a stabilizing breath. "No."

He fell silent. She saw the disappointment in his eyes. "Did you think you were?" he finally asked.

"No. I mean, there's still a chance, but I figured the odds weren't all that good, since we only did the deed that once…" She finished breathlessly.

To her surprise, he looked a little embarrassed. "Then why were you there?" he asked her calmly.

Merri shrugged. "I wanted to make sure all systems were go if and when we ever got around to…"

"Making love again."

She exhaled in relief. "Yes."

"And…?"

"I'm definitely healthy," Merri announced. "Definitely midcycle."

"Definitely ovulating," Chase presumed.

She turned bright pink.

Crinkly lines appeared at the corners of his eyes. "You are, aren't you?"

He didn't have to smile so widely. "Yes," she admitted reluctantly, knowing it would do no good to fib to a man with M.D. at the end of his name. "I'm at my prime for the next twenty-four to forty-eight hours."

He chuckled, obviously raring to go. "Were you going to tell me?"

Merri made a face. "I was thinking about it."

He made a face right back.

"I don't want you to feel like you're a stud on call or anything," Merri hurriedly said. "I mean, we may live on a ranch, but things don't work that way between you and me."

"They sure haven't lately."

She pushed herself off the stool. He took her place and tugged her onto his lap. "Do you still want a baby?" he asked, hugging her close. "*My* baby?"

Like, who else's would she want? "Yes," Merri said soberly, deciding a serious question deserved a serious answer. "I still want your baby, Chase. Very much. And…" She wreathed her arms about his neck.

"And what?"

"I want you."

MERRI'S CONFESSION WASN'T what Chase expected to hear, but it was what he needed. "I want you, too," he whispered, laying claim to her with a kiss.

Trembling, Merri kissed him back with hot, open-mouthed kisses that invited even as they incited. There was only one problem. Chase lifted his head. "When are the kids coming home?"

Merri smiled. "They aren't. I have to pick them up in town at four-thirty."

"Which means we've got less than an hour."

Her soft, sexy laughter was music to his ears. "Think we can get it done?"

He chuckled back. "I reckon." He set her down, stood and then swung her back up into his arms. "As long as we get started right away." Holding her against his chest, he strode toward the stairs. She kissed his neck, the underside of his chin, the corner of his lips, as he moved. With every touch of her mouth, blood pooled, low and strong. By the time they reached the bed, they were both breathing erratically.

He set her down and tipped her face up to his. The way she looked at him then, all soft and wanting, prodded him to risk even more—not just his body, but his heart. He tugged Merri closer and slanted his lips over hers, taking everything she had to give. And she gave him everything...

Chase inhaled the sweet fragrance of her skin and the lingering scent of her perfume, and knew he'd been welcomed into her world, fully and completely, at long last. He threaded his hands through her hair, totally immersed in the here and now, in the way her soft sweater dress clung to her slim body, the way her nipples pressed against the fabric, the way her legs parted, ever so slightly.

"Chase."

Needing more, he slipped his hands beneath her dress, shifting it higher. Sliding his palms across her tummy, he hooked his thumbs into the elastic of her tights and peeled them down. Then, kneeling, he followed their path with his lips.

She gasped and held his head in her hands. He wrapped his arms around her thighs, basking in her warmth, the silk of her skin, the way she shuddered, when he hadn't even touched her yet.

He kissed her again, loving the way she opened herself

up to him, with a purity and innocence that rocked him to his core. "You're so soft," he whispered. "So sweet."

"And needy," she teased, lifting her dress and pulling it up over her head. Smiling down at him, she undid the clasp of her bra. Lust poured through him at the sight of her pink, jutting nipples, along with the need to possess more than just her body.

With a low moan of pleasure, she drew him to his feet. His mouth found her breasts, the slope of her neck, the vulnerable hollow of her throat and then her mouth.

She kissed him again and again, already reaching for the buttons on his shirt, his fly. A short time later, they were both naked, both on the bed. She was climbing astride him. Their gazes locked. And then she was kissing him again, with a sweet deliberation. She caressed his abdomen, his thighs, touching...tempting. Until he could stand it no more, and shifted her onto her back.

Grabbing a pillow, he slid it beneath her hips. Brought her knees up and pushed her heels back, to rest against her derriere. Eyes widening, she gasped again as Chase climbed between her thighs and they slowly, deliberately became one.

Self-control evaporating, she cried out as his hands moved over her, finding every pleasure point, loving and possessing. She arched up into him, surrendering willingly. Raw need gripped them both and then they were climbing. Higher, higher still. Until they crested together and clung there, hearts pounding in unison before coming slowly, slowly back down again, to the most wonderful peace Chase had ever known in his life.

For long moments, Merri held him tightly.

Finally, she whispered, "Chase?"

"Hmm?"

"Do you think we made a baby?"

He kissed her cheek, then leaned back to gaze into her eyes. "I hope so." Because there was nothing he wanted more than another child with her, one they created on their own this time. "But if not—" he bent and kissed her again, feeling connected to her in a very fundamental way "—we'll just have to keep trying." Sighing with pure male satisfaction, he lowered his head and fused his lips to hers in a long, sensual kiss.

"A hard job, hmm?" Merri teased, the look in her eyes saying she already wanted him again.

He grinned back. "But since somebody's got to do it, it might as well be us." And then to make sure they gave it their all, he set about making love to her again.

Chapter Ten

Close to suppertime, Paige welcomed Merri and Chase into her restored Victorian home. "Don't you-all look happy. The two of you are positively glowing."

And why not, given the way she and Chase had just made love? Merri thought. As if they were in love…and always would be. Although nothing of the kind had been said, as per their earlier agreement to keep theirs a practical family arrangement, instead of a conventional romance.

"So is it true?" Paige pressed. "Or is the hospital grapevine just working overtime?"

Aware that people were still trying to figure out why she and Chase had gotten together, Merri pursed her lips. "The rumor mill is wrong. I'm not pregnant."

Chase took the gossip in stride. "We're trying, though. That's no secret."

Paige studied Chase's smile. "Sounds like fun."

It had been. Maybe too much? Wanting to steer the conversation away from their complicated relationship, Merri asked, "How have the kids been?"

"Good." Her friend smiled in turn. "They're out in the sunroom. They played with our wooden train set earlier. They couldn't stop talking about the electric one Chase set up for them."

He nodded fondly. "My old Lionel."

"It made quite an impression on Jessalyn and Jeffrey. As have you, Chase. They couldn't stop talking about how much fun it is to have a father around."

Joy lit Chase's face. "They said that?"

Paige led the way to the rear of the house. "Not in so many words. But it was 'Chase this' and 'Chase that.' Clearly, they adore you, which again is no surprise," she declared. "Kurt and I always knew you would make a great dad someday. And, of course, Merri's always been a great mom to them."

As the adults moved through the kitchen, they heard the voices of three-year-old Lindsay, Lori and Lucille, as well as those of the twins. Jeffrey was speaking loudly and authoritatively as they approached—*maybe because he was the only male in the group?* Merri wondered. "The daddy does not sleep in the same bed as the mommy. The mommy sleeps here." Jeffrey pointed to the pink bedroom in the dollhouse. "And the daddy doll sleeps here." He put the boy doll in another bedroom, on the other side of the hall.

Jessalyn was nodding in agreement. "And the twin babies sleep here," she said, putting two infant dolls in yet another bedroom.

"No," Lindsay argued, joining the melee with her two dolls clutched firmly in her little hands. "The mommy and daddy sleep together in the same bed. Like this." The other triplets nodded vigorously in support.

Jessalyn rushed to her brother's defense, saying emphatically, "The mommy and daddy do *not* sleep in the same bed. They sleep in different beds."

Merri felt her cheeks grow hot. Chase squinted. Paige managed not to look at either of them. "Hey, kids," she said with a pediatrician's gentleness, "look who's here!"

"Chase!" Jeffrey and Jessalyn exclaimed in unison. They rushed over to greet him, wrapping their arms around his legs. He hugged them back with a forearm arm around each one's shoulders.

Jeffrey gazed up at Chase with utter hero worship. "Tell them you do not sleep in the same bed as our mommy!"

Could this get any worse? Merri wondered miserably.

"Yeah," Jessalyn insisted. "Tell 'em, Chase!"

"I think the mommy and daddy dolls can sleep wherever they want to," he answered smoothly. "Together or apart."

"And I think," Paige interjected, studiously ignoring what had just been revealed by adroitly changing the subject, "that it's time for everyone to put the toys away and say goodbye."

A chorus of groans went up from all five kids as they reluctantly complied. "Do they hafta go?" Lindsay whined.

"We want to play more," Lucille said with a stomp of her ballet-slipper-clad foot.

"Maybe you can come to our house next week," Merri offered.

"Sounds like a great idea, doesn't it, girls?" Paige concurred. Mollified, the kids smiled in assent.

Merri held out her hands to the twins. "Say thank you to your hosts for having you over," she said. Dutifully, they did. Coats, caps and mittens were gathered. With promises to see each other soon, Chase and Merri escorted the twins out the door.

They stopped at the Dairy Barn for a quick bite, then headed back to the Broken Arrow. Baths and bedtime followed.

Chase met up with Merri downstairs.

He took one look at her face and knew the direction of her thoughts. "Paige isn't going to say anything."

Merri knew her friend would never knowingly hurt them. "It's humiliating enough that she heard."

Chase took her into his arms. "I think we'll get over it."

Merri exhaled slowly. "That's not the point." She looked up at him. "What are the kids saying to everyone else, at preschool?"

Once again, all that raw male power was focused on her. "You want me to ask their teacher?"

Merri flushed. "No. Of course not." She stepped away.

He shrugged and shoved his hands in the pockets of his jeans. "Then don't worry about it."

His laissez-faire attitude was driving her crazy. "How can I not? We thought the talk and speculation after I was seen at the obstetrician's office was bad. What's it going to be like when word gets around that I'm trying to get pregnant and we're not even sleeping in the same bed?"

He strolled closer, his eyes intent. Even in a rumpled shirt and jeans, with a day's growth of beard rimming his face, he looked raskishly sexy. "There's only one way to fix this. We sleep together…in the same bed and the same room from now on."

Her mouth went dry. "Chase…I…"

"I mean it, Merri." He clapsed her shoulders with his big hands. "It's time we stop testing the waters and got all the way into this marriage."

Basking in the warm familiarity of his gaze, Merri realized he made a valid point. Besides, she couldn't risk the kids coming out with anything else.

"This way," Chase continued smoothly, "whatever the kids do say will only add credence to the fact that we're serious about this marriage and have been from the first."

Merri swallowed, aware this still wasn't love. Nor was it ever likely to be except in the most casual way. "All right," she said finally. "I'll do this for you."

"For us."

Heart pounding, Merri nodded. "But there's something

else we have to do, too," she stipulated in return. "Go and see Liz first thing tomorrow, and talk to her about our concerns."

FORTUNATELY, THEIR ATTORNEY made time to see them shortly after they dropped the twins at preschool the next morning. "So what's up?" she asked.

Merri wrung her hands nervously. "I'm really worried about the public perception of our marriage, and how that might impact Judge Roy's decision."

Liz looked at Chase, to see how he was feeling. "I can understand where Merri is coming from."

Merri went on, "First, there were all the raised eyebrows when Chase's army friends showed up without warning, just a couple days after we got married. Then our awkwardness as a couple at the Thanksgiving dinner at the community center. The scene in the grocery store with the twins…"

Briefly, Chase jumped in to explain what had happened the first time he had taken the twins out on his own.

"And now," Merri continued, her misery mounting, "we just found out the twins are saying things to their preschool friends that could be misconstrued."

Liz squinted. "Such as…?"

"That there have been nights, because of Chase's schedule at the hospital, where we've been sleeping in different rooms."

Liz listened sympathetically.

"And now, because I was seen at the obstetrician's office yesterday, there are rumors that I'm pregnant."

"Are you?" the attorney asked, poker-faced.

"Not yet." Merri flushed.

Chase added seriously, "For the record—we're trying."

Liz shrugged and said nothing about the wisdom of that, either way. "Okay."

"But then I got to thinking that maybe the judge wouldn't approve of that, either." Unable to sit still a moment longer, Merri vaulted out of her chair. "What if Judge Roy decides that neither of us are good enough parents? And that I shouldn't have guardianship of the twins myself? I mean, I see on the surface that none of what we've done here makes sense to outsiders." She began to pace. "And yet Chase and I agree we're not going to rectify that by making his true paternity part of the public record. Because we think that would hurt the kids…."

Liz interjected gently, "You're in a difficult situation."

"An understatement." Chase grumbled, shoving his hands through his hair.

The lawyer regarded them both solemnly. "I understand your concerns, but the judge doesn't make a decision based on gossip, or even anything that happens around town. She rules by using the facts and data that have been submitted to the court—the financial records and employment history of both of you, your marriage license, Merri's history of guardianship to date, the wishes of the late parents and, finally, Merri's wishes to now share guardianship duties with you, Chase."

Liz paused to let her words sink in. "Judge Roy *cannot rule* based on rumors and innuendo, or even any unfortunate scenes she may have seen in the grocery store, because none of this is legally relevant to your petition."

That all sounded good. And yet… "But the judge is human and she's a parent, and by all standards, a very good parent." Practically a perfect one, Merri thought dourly.

Liz nodded. "Which is probably going to make her more understanding because she does have children."

"Then why didn't she say anything to us at the time?" Chase asked quietly, moving to stand next to Merri. "Or at least crack an understanding smile, if that was the case?"

The lawyer rocked back in her chair. "Because she didn't want to do anything that would taint the case and have it overturned on appeal."

"Oh," Merri said, catching Chase's eye. He put his hand in hers and clasped it firmly.

"The facts are," Liz continued, "you are both upstanding citizens. You've done a good job as guardian to the twins for the last four-plus years, Merri. You've managed the estate well, and the children are thriving. Everyone can see Chase is trying, and that things are getting better as time goes on. Right?"

Merri and Chase both nodded. The twins weren't calling him Daddy yet, Merri reflected silently, but they were growing more emotionally attached to him, more so every day. That much was clear.

"You're both family to these twins. You're married. And this isn't about the ranch."

"Not at all," Chase and Merri confirmed in unison.

Silence fell for several moments.

"So does this mean you think Judge Roy will rule in our favor?" Merri asked at last.

Liz leaned forward. "I can't promise you that you are going to have a good outcome."

No lawyer could, Merri knew. That would equate to having a crystal ball.

"Judge Roy has the information she requested, and I guarantee she will look it over very carefully. Meanwhile, the two of you are going to continue to do everything you can, between now and the hearing on January 3, to demonstrate that you are serious in your intent, and devoted to each other and the kids."

"Beyond that?" Chase asked, with furrowed brow.

Liz shrugged. "We all wait it out and hope for the best."

That suddenly seemed like too little, too late in the offense department. "What happens if Judge Roy denies the request?" Merri asked, needing to know—and prepare for— the worst-case scenario for her own peace of mind.

"You can appeal," Liz stated bluntly, lifting her hand. "But let's not go there, Merri. We'll cross that bridge if and when we come to it."

"What else can we do?" Chase asked, squeezing Merri's hand.

"Nothing. You have to be patient." Liz smiled gently. "I know it's hard. But it's the only thing you can do. Just keep doing the best you can by the kids, and see what happens."

MERRI LEFT THEIR ATTORNEY's office more distraught than when she'd entered. "Well, that didn't help!"

Chase put his hands on her shoulders. "It's going to be okay."

She ignored the comforting warmth radiating from his palms. "I don't know how you can say that."

He tightened his grip protectively and leaned in close. "I say it because I believe in us." Before she could do more than haul in a breath, he lowered his head and kissed her full on the mouth, not caring that they were standing in the middle of Main Street. Merri had never been one for public displays of affection, but there was no denying that the steamy embrace was working its magic and making her feel so alive.

Finally, he lifted his head. She looked up at him, dazed and aroused. And comforted, too.

"Better?" he murmured softly.

He didn't know the half of it. But she was not about to encourage him, lest he think it was okay to do this on a regular basis, especially when they had a court case coming up.

Merri cleared her throat. "You make me want to believe in dreams coming true…" And a marriage that had started out all wrong, but was beginning to feel, despite the odds, all right....

He looked deep into her eyes. "And Christmas cheer?"

Merri sighed, meeting his compelling gaze. "Definitely Christmas cheer," she murmured back.

So far this had been her best holiday season ever, despite the difficulties.

"And speaking of holiday spirit, I think we should attend the hospital staff Christmas party tomorrow evening, as a family."

Merri pulled up the calendar on her phone. "Don't you have to work?"

He nodded. "I get off at six. I'll meet you and the kids in my office. We'll go to the party together."

"Sounds good."

UNFORTUNATELY, THINGS DIDN'T work out as they had planned.

When Merri and the twins got to the hospital Saturday evening, Chase was not in his office. Kate Marten, the head of grief counseling, was. Merri took one look at the mixture of apology and regret on her face and said, "Let me guess... Chase isn't coming." So much for their plans to present a united front to the community at large.

"He's with a patient. It will be a while. I told him I'd escort you and the twins to the party in the meantime."

This was all part of being a surgeon's wife, Merri told herself sternly. She pushed her disappointment aside and smiled with all the graciousness she could muster. "Sounds good. Thank you." She gathered the twins, who had been looking around curiously, close to her side.

The four of them went back out into the hall that led from the annex of doctor's offices to the main hospital. Merri couldn't help but think about the last time she had seen Kate there. It had been shortly after she and Chase had said their vows, in the LCH chapel. The psychologist had offered her services, on behalf of the hospital, in any way they needed. Neither of them had taken her up on her offer.

"So how have you been?" Kate asked casually.

"Very busy." *Falling hard for my handsome husband.* Merri slanted the older woman a look. "You?"

"The holidays are always busy for our department."

"I imagine so," Merri murmured. "Grief can hit you pretty hard around the Christmas season. It did me for several years after—" mindful of the twins, she chose her words carefully "—our loss."

"But it's better now?" the counselor asked gently.

With joy welling up inside her, Merri admitted, "I have a lot to look forward to these days. A lot to be thankful for, too."

"That's good to hear." Kate paused at the door of the staff lounge, which had been converted into a winter wonderland. Snowflakes hung from the ceiling. Garlands of white decorated the walls. A thronelike chair sat next to the beautifully decorated Christmas tree. Festively dressed children and adults were already enjoying the sumptuous holiday buffet that had been set out.

Merri's friend Emily came over to say hello, and Kate eased away into the crowd of partygoers.

"I didn't realize you were going to be here tonight," Merri said.

"My café is catering the event. Dylan was tapped to play a very important role, too. You know. Lots of ho, ho, ho and Christmas cheer and all that." Emily inclined her head slightly toward the Saint Nicholas throne.

"Oh." Merri grinned.

"He's a little nervous." Emily chuckled and continued speaking in code. "He's never done it before. But the staff thought it would be better to have someone largely unrecognizable to the tiny folk."

Merri chuckled, too. "Good thinking."

Jessalyn tugged on her hand. "Mommy, where's our daddy?"

"Yeah," Jeffrey said, pulling on her other hand. "You told us Chase was going to be here tonight!"

"I know," Merri commiserated gently, wishing she did not have to be the bearer of bad news on such a happy occassion. "But—"

"Hey! There he is!" Jessalyn bounced up and down. "There's our daddy!"

She pulled free of Merri at the same time her brother did. The two raced for Chase, who was still clad in blue surgical scrubs and a white coat. "Chase! Chase!" they both shouted, as a few eyebrows rose.

Merri knew what the adults were thinking.

Shouldn't the twins be addressing Chase as "Daddy" now, instead of by his given name?

He hoisted a child in each arm and lifted them up against his broad chest. "Jessalyn! Jeffrey!" he teased, in the same excited tone.

The kids beamed up at him just as bells jingled in the hallway. Seconds later, a bearded Santa Claus strode in, clad in the traditional red velvet garb. "Ho, ho, ho!" Dylan Reeves boomed, eyes twinkling behind the wire-rimmed glasses. "And Merry Christmas!" He set down his pack and stood, hands on his hips, gazing at all the wide-eyed children gathered around him. "Who wants to be first to tell Santa Claus what you want more than anything in this world?"

Dylan pointed at Jessalyn and Jeffrey. "How about you?" He sat down and held out his arms.

For a moment, Merri didn't think the children were going

to approach him. Then Chase bent his head and whispered something in their ears. They grinned, and wriggled to be let down. When Chase set them on the floor they marched over to Santa Claus, one by one whispering something in his ear.

Dylan looked surprised. "That's what you want?" he asked.

Jessalyn and Jeffrey glanced at each other and nodded vigorously.

"Well, that's a mighty fine wish," Dylan boomed, with a wink and a nod. "I'll see what I can do to make it happen."

"DYLAN WOULDN'T TELL YOU, either?" Merri asked Chase hours later, as they got ready for bed.

"He said, and I quote, 'I think that's the kind of thing you want to hear straight from them.'"

"But the twins wouldn't tell us what they told 'Santa'!" Merri protested, hand over her heart.

Clad in a pair of low-slung pajama pants, Chase picked up his toothbrush. "Dylan is sure it will come out eventually, when the time is right. Say, on Christmas morning."

Merri tore her eyes from the sculpted contours of his bare chest. "Then it will be too late. We won't have gotten them whatever it is that their little hearts desire more than anything in this world."

He handed her the toothpaste tube. "Dylan said it's not the kind of thing you can buy."

Together, they brushed and rinsed. Merri straightened, wiping her mouth on a towel. "Then how are we going to get it for them?"

"Good question." Chase dabbed a bit of paste from the corner of her lip with his fingertip. Silence fell and then he shook his head. "I thought parenting was supposed to be easy."

Merri switched off the light and followed him out of the bathroom. "According to what book?"

Together, they walked over to the bed. Chase shrugged. "The good parents make it look easy."

Merri climbed beneath the covers. "Don't sell yourself short, Chase. You've been an amazing dad to the twins."

He shrugged and joined her, leaning against the pillows. "You think so?"

"I know so." She snuggled closer, insinuating her leg between his. "They love having you around. They were really disappointed when they thought you weren't going to make it to the party tonight."

He wrapped his arms around her and sighed deeply.

"I was disappointed, too. But I got there."

"You sure did."

Silence fell again. He continued stroking her hair, then pressed a kiss on top of her head. Much lower, she felt him stirring.

"You know, chances are you're still ovulating," he murmured.

Merri's pulse picked up. They'd made love every day since she'd visited the doctor. And though she had heard that sometimes men grew weary of the baby-making routine, Chase seemed no more tired of her than she was of him. In fact...

She let her fingers caress the flat, silky expanse of his abdomen. "You really want to...?"

He caught her by the waist and shifted her upward, until she was cozily ensconced over him. "I do," he whispered tenderly, kissing her.

Merri smiled and returned the caress with all she had. "Well, then, it's settled," she said, slipping her arms about his neck. "Because I do, too."

Chapter Eleven

The twins barreled into the kitchen just as Merri took the last blueberry pancake off the griddle. "Mommy, how come our daddy is yelling?" Jeffrey demanded.

Merri wrinkled her brow. "What do you mean, yelling?"

"Like this!" He looked at his sister, and they yelped in unison. "Do you think he got a boo-boo in the shower?"

A faint trickle of alarm went through Merri. "Did it sound like he did?"

The two shrugged. "I dunno," Jeffrey said.

"Was the water running?"

They nodded affirmatively.

"Then what happened?" Merri turned off the griddle. "Did Chase stop yelling?"

"Yes, but first he said some of the words we're not supposed to say."

"And then what?"

Jessalyn blinked. "It was real real quiet."

"Except for the water," Jeffrey added seriously. "'Cause it was still on."

Merri knelt down to their eye level. "Did you ask Chase if he was okay?"

Jessalyn scoffed. "You told us not to bother a grown-up in the bathroom 'less it was an emergency. And we didn't have an emergency!"

Did Chase have an emergency? Merri hoped not. Bathroom accidents could be lethal, and if he wasn't talking, that could mean he had fallen and hit his head.... Feigning calm, she guided the twins into their chairs. "You two sit down and eat your pancakes. I'll go check on your daddy."

"Should you take him a Band-Aid?" Jeffrey called after her.

"I have some upstairs. I'm sure it will be fine." Merri walked as far as the hall, then dashed on up the stairs, silenting berating herself all the way. This was what she got for allowing Chase, who had clearly been dead on his feet after an eighteen-hour shift to get cleaned up and try to stay awake long enough to have breakfast with the twins before they went off to preschool.

She should have told him his health was more important, and sent him straight to bed. The kids would have understood.

Merri burst into the master bedroom, raced through it and threw open the bathroom door.

The shower had stopped, she realized belatedly. Chase was standing there, naked as could be, dripping wet.

"What happened?" He stepped out of the glass door.

Merri was hit with a blast of cool air. And the impact of gazing at her sexy-as-could-be mate in the altogether. Flushing and terribly aroused, she explained, "The twins said you were yelping in distress!"

Chase looked embarrassed. "They heard that?"

She imitated the sounds the twins had made.

He chuckled. "That was me, all right." He lazily rubbed himself down with a towel. His flat male nipples were erect, as the rest of him was beginning to be, she noted, despite the goose bumps standing out on his arms and legs.

Reluctantly, Merri dragged her gaze back to his face. "Did you run out of hot water?"

"Yes. And then no." He ran a towel over the day's growth of beard on his face. "And then yes. And then no."

She smacked her forehead with the flat of her hand. "Oh, no."

"Oh, yes…" Towel around his waist, Chase closed the distance and hauled her against him. He smelled good. Like soap. And mint. And man.

Merri apologized with a wince. "I forgot I had the washer on! I always put in a load first thing, before I start breakfast."

His eyes roved her face appreciatively. "I could tell it was something like that." He ran a hand down her spine, drawing her closer still.

"I'm not used to having a man around." Merri's breasts pressed against the hard, damp muscles of his chest.

"I could tell that, too." Chase's hands slid lower and cupped her derrierre. "Although I can't say I'm sorry about that." He kissed her temple, her cheek, her ear. "I like being your one and only."

And I like being yours. Much more of this and she would really fall in love with him.…

Merri swallowed, noting the sudden parched feeling in her throat. "Forgive me?" she asked.

"Depends." His wicked grin widened as he pulled her up on tiptoe, so she was pressed even more intimately against him. "Are you going to kiss me and make it all better?"

"Well," she whispered playfully, "when you put it that way…" She linked her arms around his shoulders, closed her eyes.

"Mommy!"

"What are you doing, and where is Chase's boo-boo?" The twins' voices echoed loudly and impatiently behind her.

Merri knew what part needed to be eased. It was pressed up against her and hidden beneath the towel. Busted by the most diligent and effective of chaperones, she dropped her arms and turned carefully, so her back was against his chest, her hips nestled against the proof of his desire.

Chase wrapped his arms around her waist, holding her close. He lowered his head and pressed his lips to her hair. "We were going to kiss," he explained.

"Yuck!" the twins said in unison.

"I know." Chase regarded them solemnly. "So it's a good thing you came up here and interrupted us, otherwise who knows what might have happened?"

The children wrinkled their noses, clearly perplexed while Merri stifled her laughter.

"Did you get an owie?" Jessalyn demanded eventually, coming closer.

"No," Chase told them sincerely. "I'm sorry if it sounded like I did."

"We ran out of hot water again," Merri explained. "Everything is fine."

"Oh."

She shepherded the twins toward the door. "Our breakfasts are getting cold. Daddy—" she cast a look over her shoulder, making no effort to hide her affection "—we'll see you downstairs, okay?"

Chase nodded and gave her a look that said he intended to finish what they had started. Jovially, he called, "Be right there, kids! As soon as I get dressed."

"BYE! HAVE A GREAT DAY at school!"

"We'll see you later!"

Merri and Chase waved as the car carrying the preschoolers drove off.

He walked back inside with her. "So," he concluded huskily, "you were worried about me."

Merri shut and locked the door behind them. "Of course

I was worried." She made a comical face. "The twins made it sound like you had fallen and couldn't get up."

His belly laugh electrified the air. "So naturally," he concluded, deadpan, "you told them to stay put, and came to my rescue."

"Well." Merri shrugged and met his eyes. "You are my husband." More so every day.

He ran his palm over his unshaved jaw. "Speaking of marital duties…"'

Merri quirked her lips. "Were we?"

"We're about to." His expression innocent, he swung her up onto the kitchen counter and moved in, trapping her with his arms.

Merri's heart began a slow, heavy beat. Chase smiled. "Now, where were we earlier, when we were interrupted?" He undid one button on her blouse, then another. Gazed down at her cleavage. "Oh. I think I remember…."

"Chase…"

He undid several more buttons. "We haven't had nearly enough time alone." Easing the blouse from her body, he whispered, "I vote we take advantage of this…."

The kiss that followed ramped up her desire and curled her toes. Eventually, he lifted his head. "So what do you say?"

Merri sucked in a breath, aware she had zero willpower where her husband was concerned. She rubbed the moisture from his lips. "That you're a hard man to say no to."

His next smile was even more devastating. Chase took her hand, and pressed it over his manhood. "I'm a hard man, period. And I have been since you walked in on me."

Merri checked him out. "That's not good."

He shifted his weight. "It can be. At times like now."

Oh, my. "Chase."

"Merri…"

She smiled, knowing that he knew he had turned her on in a major way. She kissed the tip of his nose, his cheek, his jaw. Ran her free hand down his chest. "We should go upstairs."

His eyes turned opaque. He lifted her hand from the most masculine part of him and kissed the back of it. "We'll get there. Eventually." His eyes darkened all the more. "But first…"

Chase undid the clasp of her bra, which went the way of her blouse. She trembled, watching as he ran his fingers across the smooth skin of her abdomen, over her ribs, then palmed her breasts. He groaned at her responsiveness.

Merri rested her forearms on his shoulders and gazed up at him. "You make me feel so good."

His lids lowered to half-mast. "At last, you've discovered my plan," he teased, covering her mouth with his once again. Merri's pulse skipped ahead, into a fast, hard rhythm as he kissed her, his body unyielding. No longer willing to wait for a bed, she palmed his shoulders, the corded muscles of his back, the smooth curve of his buttocks.

Chase moaned. Smiling, she brought her hands around to the front of his soft gray sweats and slid her fingers beneath the waistband. He moaned again as she pushed it down, caught the band of his briefs and slid her fingers beneath that, too. His skin there was warm and covered with crisp hair. Lower still was the satin hardness she had admired earlier. She closed her fingers around him, wanting, needing.

"Not yet." He caught her wrist, his voice hoarse and unsteady.

She clutched at him, already spiraling. "Yes.…" *Yes! Yes!*

"You're not ready."

Merri felt the throbbing deep within her, the slipperiness between her thighs. "I beg to differ with you there, pardner…" she argued, her voice soft and thick.

Smiling with lascivious intent, Chase eased open the front of her jeans, lowered the zipper. "But you will be," he promised, lifting her long enough to push the denim down and then off.

Cool air assaulted Merri's skin. She trembled as he set her down again, positioning her legs so they were wrapped around his waist. He kissed her once more, stroking her with his hands, ever so tenderly. Merri shuddered in response and opened even more, desire sweeping through her in powerful waves.

Chase lifted her partially off the counter, murmuring encouragement all the while. Just when she thought she couldn't stand it anymore, he ended the passionate kiss and lowered his head to her breasts. Excitement surged through her as his lips became as busy as his hands, laving, adoring, inciting. Deliberately, he moved her against him, shifting her back and forth, driving her out of her mind, even with his clothes between them. Need overcame her, and everything in her tightened and peaked. She finally let out an exultant cry and trembled in release.

Chase's eyes were hot and his smile was tight when she slowly came back down to earth. Transfixed at the sight of him, so hard and hot and ready, she reached for the hem of his T-shirt, dragged it up over his head and tossed it to the floor. He watched her, clearly liking her plan, when she drew his sweatpants and briefs the rest of the way down his thighs. He kicked them off, away.

Merri caught him by the shoulders and brought him close, wrapping her legs around him until she was straddling him, and he was… right where she wanted him. This time she let herself look into his eyes as he slid home, going deep, going slow. Emotion shimmered through her.

She wasn't sure she had felt married before.

She did now.

She wasn't sure she had felt loved before.

She did now.

She wasn't sure he'd felt loved, either.

But the way he was looking at her, so avidly, so openly, told her that in this moment, he did. And really, Merri thought as she took his head in her hands and brought her mouth to his, that was all they needed.

"DON'T GO." CHASE CAUGHT Merri's hand before she could leave the bed, and pulled her back into his arms. He kissed her neck, behind her ear, leaving trails of fire and need in his wake.

Merri shut her eyes, basking briefly in the erotic glow the two of them created every time they were together like this. "Believe me." She sighed, absorbing his warmth and strength. "I would like nothing better than to stay, but I have to go."

He slid his hands down her hips. "Why?"

Much more and he'd have her begging. Merri tried—unsuccessfully—to wriggle free. "Because if I don't I'll stay here all day."

He smiled as if he'd won a prize. "So?"

"And you won't get any sleep. And as your wife," she continued archly, tingling even as she slipped from his light, easy grip, "one of my duties is to make sure you get the rest you need. So people won't be saying things like, 'Have you seen Chase Armstrong? Boy, that fella sure isn't getting any shut-eye.'"

Chase threw back his head and let out a raucous laugh. "They'd probably just figure it was because I was on my honeymoon with my very hot and lovely wife."

Merri grinned despite herself at the image that conjured up. She sat beside him and stroked the crisp, curling hair on his chest. "You can be really ornery, you know that?"

He ran his eyes over her possessively, admiring her naked form. "Someone currently in this room brings it out in me." Then he bent to kiss her knee. "And speaking of that person—you still haven't told me what you want for Christmas."

Selecting the right gift was hard under normal circumstances. In this instance…? She shook off the question, letting him know that he didn't have to give her a present. "I have everything I want and need." *Well, almost,* she amended silently.

He studied her eyes. "Except a baby."

Merri smiled. "I think we just worked on that." Although from what she knew, the ovulation period was either well over or fading fast. She looked at him, knowing generosity should go both ways. "What do you want for Christmas?"

Devilry lit his eyes. "Besides more lovemaking?"

"There must be something you want and don't have."

"I really can't think of anything, now that I've got you and the twins."

"Except…"

His expression turned wistful.

"…the fact they aren't yet calling you Daddy," Merri guessed.

He exhaled. "At least they've accepted that I *am* their daddy."

Merri gathered up her clothes. "It would be nice to have them call you something other than Chase."

Arms folded behind his head, he lay back on the pillows and watched her dress. "I asked Kate Marten about that. I figured she would know, since she's had a lot of experience dealing with kids, moving out of one situation and into another, so to speak."

Merri came closer, still buttoning. "And?"

He shifted over so she could sit down and put on her

socks. "She said it will happen when the kids are ready, and not before."

Merri turned, concluding, "So we have to be patient."

Chase nodded. He took her face in his hands and gave her another sweet and loving kiss. "Which, as it turns out, is not such a bad thing. As long as we're together."

Chapter Twelve

Chase had just sat down to go over the chart of a patient he had operated on, when his cell phone vibrated.

"Going to be one of those days, hmm?" Paige commented, from the other side of the conference table.

Luckily for him, it wasn't anything that would take him back to the O.R. He showed the screen to his colleague.

Wordlessly, Paige checked out the photo of his six vacationing army friends, who'd been visiting the Grand Ole Opry in Tennessee. All were decked out in Santa hats and grinning broadly, next to a hand-lettered sign, held by Starr, that said Hi, Chase!

Having just come out of surgery herself, Paige paused to make a notation on a chart. "You still getting those?"

He nodded. "Every time the ladies hit a particularly exciting landmark or destination."

His colleague got up, walked to the fridge in the corner of the staff lounge and took out two bottles of sparkling water. Returning, she handed one to him. "Merri okay with that?"

Chase wondered if Paige was thinking about what the twins had said—about him and Merri sleeping in separate beds. Something in her inscrutable expression hinted that she was. Not about to go there, he sat back and uncapped the bottle. "Sure." He lifted it and took a long drink. "Why wouldn't she be?"

The pediatrician shrugged, her concern for her longtime friend evident. "They're all awfully pretty."

Chase was growing tired of everyone telling him how to manage his marriage. He didn't need or want their advice, well-meant or not. "Merri understands they're just good friends."

Another silence fell, followed by a lift of Paige's brow.

Chase had never been one to explain himself to others. In this case, to protect Merri, he made an exception. "Relationships in field hospitals can get pretty intense."

Paige took another look at the photo on the screen and relaxed slightly. "And just like when you're out of medical school or residency, they fade."

"Merri knows that, too." Chase picked up his pen.

"Still, that kind of thing can be easily misinterpreted."

Did she think that was why he and Merri had been sleeping apart in the beginning? Not that it mattered, since he wasn't about to kiss and tell.

"Merri knows it's only temporary. They're all headed back overseas a few days after Christmas."

"And Merri's not jealous."

Chase thought about the passionate, unrestrained way the two of them had been making love, the happiness they had found. "She understands how I feel about her."

"Good." Paige inclined her head toward the picture on his smart phone. "'Cause if she didn't, pal, you might be in trouble."

WITH CHASE TIED UP IN SURGERY all day, Merri decided to get a little shopping done. So, after she picked the kids up at preschool, she took them to the Dairy Barn for lunch and a talk. "Now that you're older, it's time you realized that Christmas isn't just about getting presents," she said seriously, acutely aware there were only ten shopping days left. "It's about giving something, too."

"We know that, Mommy!" Jessalyn dipped her chicken tender into barbecue sauce. "That's how come we already made you something at school."

"Want us to tell you what it is?" Jeffrey asked eagerly. "Because—"

"Uh, no." Merri reached over and playfully covered their mouths with her hand. "You need to surprise me." She dropped her arm and sat back.

The twins nodded seriously. "Okay," Jessalyn replied.

Then Jeffrey added, "We won't tell you we made you a flowerpot and a picture frame that says I Love You, Mommy."

Not about to let on he had just unwittingly given everything way, Merri kept herself from cracking a smile. "Good. Anyway, back to what I was saying. Now that Chase is your daddy, you need to do something nice for him, too."

"We can't," Jessalyn said.

"Yeah." Jeffrey muched on a fry. "We're all done making presents at school."

"Well, that doesn't mean you can't make him something just as nice at home, while he's at work," Merri countered.

"Okay, then, we'll make him a new Lionel train, because he really likes them."

"That's a little complicated."

They looked at her expectantly. "You can help us," Jeffrey said.

Merri finished chewing her burger. "I meant complicated for me, too."

Jessalyn leaned forward importantly. "But we have to get him a new train, because he likes trains and that's what he wants."

There was no faulting that logic. "How about this?" Merri

paused to make sure she had their attention. "After we finish our lunch, we'll go over to the arts and crafts store and pick out a couple of those wooden trains that need decorating, and you two can paint them. Then Daddy can take the trains to work and put them on his desk so he'll have a reminder of you there."

"Okay," they replied happily.

Merri drew a breath, ready to tackle something much more sensitive. "And as long as we're on the subject of Daddy...don't you think it's time you started calling him Daddy?"

More frowns appeared. "That's not his name. His name is Chase," Jeffrey argued.

Patience. "I know you've always called him that." They'd never even wanted to say Uncle. "But now it's different."

Their frowns deepened. "No, it's not. That's still his name. Everybody calls him that," Jessalyn stated.

Merri inhaled and tried again. "My name is Merri, but you call me Mommy."

"Because you are our mommy."

"And Chase is your daddy," Merri reminded them gently.

"But that's not his name...."

Eventually, finally, Merri decided not to make an issue of it. Maybe Kate was right. It would happen when the twins were ready. And not one day before.

"You can't be serious!" Emily said the following afternoon, stopping by their table in the café, where Chase and Dylan sat poring over the sales literature Dylan had picked up for the busy physician. "You can't give Merri that for Christmas!"

Chase had to give her something. And judging by all the whispering the twins had been doing, and the way Merri was constantly and humorously shushing them, everyone else had a jump on him in that department.

"It's a good gift," he argued. Given how happy Merri and the kids had made him, he wanted to make sure Merri had something she would really like.

"Maybe for a non-occasion…" Dylan reluctantly agreed with his wife.

"But for your first Christmas together?" Emily topped off each of their coffees. "You've got to get her something that says how you feel about her."

A little offended, Chase pointed to the picture in front of him. "This *does* say how I feel."

Merri's friend rolled her eyes. "Maybe about the ranch, and her not doing a good enough job taking care of it."

Chase's spirits fell. He took another look. "Oh." He swore silently. "I see your point."

"I think you should still get it, given what you've told me about the issue," Dylan advised. "Just not as your primary gift, but as, um, a stocking stuffer."

"In that sense it would be okay," Emily agreed, after thinking about it for a second. "In fact, I'm sure Merri would appreciate it, if it was given in humor."

"Well, it's not like I was going to present it with all the fanfare of a new car," Chase retorted mildly.

"Cars are out, too. It's such a guy gift. No woman wants to get a car." Emily patted her husband's shoulder affectionately, then sashayed off to serve another customer.

Admiring the easy way husband and wife interacted, Chase turned back to his friend. "What are you getting Emily for Christmas?"

Dylan cut into his chicken-fried steak. "A new custom-made saddle with her name engraved on it."

Chase blinked. "You call that romantic?"

He grinned. "For a woman who likes to ride mustangs

as much as I do, it's a darn good gift. But I'm throwing in a little perfume and a negligee and stuff like that, too, that shall go unmentioned to anyone but the two of us. Just make sure whatever you give Merri says ROMANCE in capital letters."

Chase left the Daybreak Café and returned to the hospital, thinking about his friend's advice.

There was no doubt Emily and Dylan were happily married. Three years in and the two still acted like newlyweds.

Chase wanted the same result. Which got him thinking. Maybe there was a way to give Merri the romance she had been deprived of, after all.

"WHAT DO YOU MEAN I HAVE to meet you at your office in the hospital annex promptly at six-thirty?" Merri said four days later. The truth was, she was feeling a little out of sorts. Unusually tired. Bloated. *Pregnant...?* Pushing the wishful thinking aside—she was not going to count her chickens before they hatched—she drew a deep breath and waited for Chase to go on.

"I thought we'd go out for dinner this evening."

Merri would like nothing better than to have a meal in a candlelit restaurant, seated across from her handsome new husband. Especially since they'd never actually been on a real date.

It was all either family time or hot wild sex in bed.

"I appreciate the idea, but the kids just had their last day of preschool before the holiday break. They're pretty tired. I don't think they'll be able to handle a dinner out without melting down."

"I figured as much, but I've seen to that, too. Paige and Kurt said they'd take the twins. All you have to do is drop them off at their house in town on the way to meet me."

Again, Merri yearned for a real date. With adult conversation. A relaxing dinner, where she didn't have to cut up anyone else's food. She'd also like time to get ready at leisure. Maybe take a bubble bath, go to the salon, get her hair done. "You're sure we can't do this some other night?" *When I have time to prepare and can really knock your socks off?*

"You know what they say. Never put off till tomorrow what you can do today... I'll see you in a little bit, okay?"

Merri sighed and put down the phone. Luckily for her, the kids were surprisingly cooperative about getting ready to go back out. Forty-five minutes later she had dropped them off and was headed into Chase's office.

The waiting room was empty. No surprise, since his staff had gone home for the day. It was, Merri soon discovered, just the two of them. And Chase was wearing a suit and tie. The same dark suit and tie he had worn when they got married in the hospital chapel, as it happened.

She looked down at her casual jeans and sweater with regret. "You didn't tell me we were dressing up. I assumed we were going to one of the restaurants in town."

"We are, but I thought it would be nice, since tonight is our first-month anniversary, to put forth a little extra effort."

Oh, no! Merri pressed her fingers to her lips, aghast. "I totally forgot."

Those crinkles appeared at the corners of his eyes. "You're surprised I remembered."

"Well, yes, I—I guess I am." When did she start stammering? She hadn't been this nervous around him since he'd come back to town. But he hadn't looked so inscrutably mysterious since then, either.

Chase smiled wryly and scratched his head. "I guess I'm going to have to do better in the romance department."

"Trust me. You've been doing just fine." Merri had never been so head-over-heels for any man. The fact she was married to him just made it so much better.

He held up a hand. "Not to worry. I brought something from your closet…" He produced the tea-length navy dress and delicate white cardigan she had worn when they'd said their vows.

"You know what that is."

"I do. And for the record, I love the way you look in it."

He hadn't said he loved *her,* just the way she looked. Still, it was something. Merri shook her head. "You really are full of surprises this evening."

"Need help changing?"

If he helped they might end up making love on his office floor. And while that could be incredibly sexy, it wouldn't be appropriate. Merri didn't want to have to worry about a janitor walking in on them. Besides, Kurt and Paige could watch the kids for only so long before bedtime, so they better get a move on.

Merri shook her head and smiled. "I'll just be a minute."

When she walked back out, Chase was waiting for her. He had a medium-size silver gift box in his hand.

"What's that?"

He sat on the edge of his desk and pulled her toward him. "An early Christmas present."

Merri struggled with another stab of regret as she perched on his inner thigh. "I haven't gotten you anything yet."

"It's okay." He looked at her affectionately. "I want you to open this."

Merri's heart skipped a beat. "Now?"

"Yep." The sexy smile reached his eyes. "Right here. Right now."

Swallowing against the building ache in her throat, Merri undid the bow and lifted the lid. She blinked in surprise when she discovered a small, red velvet box surrounded by shiny gold tissue paper. "What is it?"

Innocence glimmered in his eyes. "Don't know. You'll have to look and see."

Merri gingerly opened the jewelry box. Inside was a diamond solitaire ring that was a perfect match for the platinum wedding rings she and Chase already wore.

The affection in his eyes deepened. "I thought you should have an engagement ring."

Tears filled Merri's eyes at the unexpected and truly lavish gesture. "Oh, Chase," she whispered, studying the sparkling diamond. "It's beautiful."

Relief mingled with the happiness on his face. "I didn't want to wait one more day."

With his help, Merri slipped it on. And for the first time, she felt married in the way she had always wanted—in the romantic sense. Emotion welled. The tears she'd been holding back spilled over her lashes, and she stood up to hug him fiercely. "You've made me so happy," Merri whispered thickly.

He hugged her back. "That goes both ways."

They paused to kiss, deeply and tenderly. Reluctantly, he drew back. "Much as I hate to say it, we'd better get moving if you want to have time to show that off," he teased.

She slanted him a curious look. "Where are we going?"

Chase led her toward the door. "Somewhere I can hold you in my arms."

They fell into step companionably. "The bed-and-breakfast just outside of town?"

He chuckled. "Good idea. But no."

As it turned out, they only had to walk down Main Street.

"The Lone Star Dance Hall?" Merri paused in front of the popular restaurant, which looked crowded. Vehicles spilled out of the lot, and onto the street. Inside, it appeared as if people were standing shoulder to shoulder.

Chase tucked a strand of hair behind her ear. "I remember it being one of your favorites when you were younger."

Merri loved to two-step and line-dance. She just hadn't done it in forever. "It is. It's sweet of you to remember."

Chase smiled and took her hand in his. Together, they walked in, and Merri got her second big shock of the night when the country and western band struck up a lively Texas version of the Wedding March.

"Surprise!" Chase murmured in her ear. "You've just been gifted with a reception."

And then on cue, all their close friends and their very nicely garbed twins shouted, "Congratulations, Chase and Merri!"

Chapter Thirteen

"You know, you don't have to keep looking at me that way," Merri murmured a bit later.

Chase took her hand in his and led her onto the floor for the first dance of the evening. And their first official dance as husband and wife. "What way?" he murmured sexily.

Joy bubbled up inside her. "Like this is the best night of your entire life."

Chase held her even closer. "It *is* the best night of my entire life." He smiled. "So far."

"Meaning what?" Merri teased, enjoying having her body pressed intimately against his. "You expect things to get even better?" How was that even possible?

He looked deep into her eyes. "I do. I think every day we spend together is going to be happier and more fulfilling than the last."

Merri grinned up at him. "Ever the optimist, aren't you?"

Chase kissed her temple. "When it comes to you and me, I have every reason to have hope and faith." And, as it turned out, he wasn't the only one who thought the two of them had only good days ahead. Everyone in the packed dance hall stopped by throughout the evening to offer similar sentiments. But what meant the most to them were the words from the hospital's chief counselor.

"I'd like to offer my congratulations, as well as an apology for my earlier misinterpretation of the situation," Kate said when the party had finally wound down and Merri and Chase were in the process of packing up and getting ready to go home.

Kate sent a fond glance toward Chase, who was corralling the still-energetic twins into their coats and hats, while Merri organized their mountain of wedding gifts. "I was wrong to think your marriage might be ill-advised. It's obvious the two of you are very much in love."

Merri paused, not sure how to respond to that. Thanks to Chase and the effort he'd put into their belated wedding reception, the night had been wildly romantic, with a professional photographer documenting it all. A sumptuous dinner had been followed by champagne toasts and wedding cake, laughter and dancing, and even the occasional surprisingly passionate kiss.

Chase had given Merri the reception of her dreams, and memories of their evening together would last a lifetime. But as for actual love? That was something she and Chase hadn't sought or even begun to discuss.

As Kate's husband, computer technology mogul Sam McCabe, joined them, Kate continued stacking gifts into neat piles, for easier transporting, "I just want you and Chase to know that we could not be happier for you."

Merri smiled as she loaded presents onto a cart. Appreciating the candor, she replied, "I realize our wedding may have seemed very quick and untraditional."

Kate smiled up at her husband of many years. "Yes, well, once upon a time, Sam and I were a surprise to everyone, too."

He laughed and squeezed her hand. "Including, as it happens, the two of us."

Merri identified with that notion, all right. She hadn't expected to have a hot, wild, passionate relationship with

Chase, never mind start to fall in love with him. But both were happening....

"The point is," Kate continued, "the foundation of every happy family is the strong love and enduring relationship between the parents."

Her husband nodded in agreement. "You can't have a successful family without that."

The couple helped Merri steer the loaded carts toward the door. "It's obvious you and Chase have something very special and unique," Kate said.

But was it love? Merri wondered. She knew how she was beginning to feel. She knew Chase desired her and enjoyed being with her and the kids. That he loved the twins was also evident. But did he love her—in the way that Kate and Sam had been talking about?

Would Chase ever care for her that way? And what would happen in the long run if he didn't? Would a one-sided emotion be enough to sustain them?

"WHAT WERE YOU TALKING ABOUT with Kate and her husband this evening?" Chase asked later, after they had put the very sleepy twins to bed.

Merri closed their bedroom door and filled him in on the conversation.

He couldn't say he was surprised. "I figured she'd come around," he admitted with a great deal of satisfaction. "Everyone would, given a little time. When they realized we weren't behaving recklessly..."

Merri nodded, looking comforted, too, by the outpouring of love and good wishes they had received. "It felt good, having the community support us that way."

Chase knew now how sensitive she was to the opinion of others. He was glad the wedding reception had made her feel better about their situation.

Merri unknotted his tie and pulled it off. "I don't know where to begin to thank you," she whispered emotionally. "It really was an incredible party."

And she'd been an incredible bride.

She looked so beautiful. Even more so than she had on their wedding day. And that was saying something.

"And the ring," she said softly. "It just makes our union all the more official."

Was that why she thought he had given it to her? Chase wondered in alarm. For appearances sake?

To his disappointment, it seemed so.

Wary of pushing her too hard, too fast, Chase reined in his quickly escalating feelings. The two of them had made a deal—to have a union based on friendship, co-parenting and sex. He had to stick to that. At least for now. Maybe in time more would be possible, but for right now they both needed to be grateful for all they had, which was a lot.

He cleared his throat. "You deserve it, Merri, and so much more." He watched as she took off her cardigan, then her dress. She slipped into the bathroom, returned in just a robe. "You've been a great wife to me. A *great* wife. And a great mother to our kids."

Merri smiled and glided closer. Their gazes meshed and she searched his eyes. "Thank you. You've been a great husband, and a great dad."

Silence stretched between them. Chase had no idea if she was ever going to want anything more than what they had right now. But he knew what he wanted to have happen. And to get there, he would need to do a lot more work on his half of the relationship.

Smiling, he toyed with the belt on her robe. "Technically, it's not our wedding night."

She undid the knot then ever so slowly released the ends. "I guess it's not."

Damn, he was hard already. "But we are still on our honeymoon." He opened her robe all the way.

She was naked. Incredibly beautiful and hot. And waiting. For him. To catch up.

She let him go and moved back, to lounge against the bureau, hands braced on either side of her, robe open.

More than ready to join her, he held her eyes as he stripped off his shirt, kicked off his shoes and shucked his pants.

Naked, too, he sauntered toward her.

Eyes glittering mischievously, she tilted her head and picked up the threads of their conversation. "I don't know, Doc, if we can still be on our honeymoon after a month."

He slid his hands inside her robe. Her skin was as hot as he was. He kissed his way down her throat, to the sensitive spot at the base of her neck. "Maybe we'll always be on our honeymoon."

She sighed and leaned closer, her nipples beading against his chest. She turned her head so their lips met, and kissed him back, until both of them were trembling. "I think I could live with that," she whispered.

"So could I." Chase carried her to the vanity and sat down with her on his lap. "Ever feel like it's Christmas already?" he asked, as he finished unwrapping her.

Merri smiled. "Every day."

Aware that she needed some serious loving—they both did—after the momentous month they'd had, Chase set about claiming her as his. She did the same for him, rocking against him, and urging him on, even as he surged into her, entering and withdrawing in shallow strokes that had them both panting and moaning for more.

They drew it out as long as possible, savoring every second, and when they'd finally reached their peak and were drifting slowly, inevitably down again, he held her while she cuddled against him.

An unimaginable tenderness swept through him. Chase knew it had been only a matter of weeks that they'd been together, but he could no longer imagine his life without her.

He sensed she felt the same.

Whether she knew it yet or not, it was a lot more than simple honor, or a desire to do the right thing, keeping him with her and the kids.

Some unions were just meant to be.

Theirs was one of them.

THE DAY AFTER THEIR RECEPTION was challenging, to say the least. With Chase at the hospital, Merri had her hands full.

"You said our daddy was going to be home for dinner!" Jeffrey grumbled.

Merri helped her son on with his coat and knelt to zip up the front. The extra excitement and late hours the evening before, and an unusually short nap that afternoon, had turned both twins cranky. Merri hoped an afternoon ride on their tricycles would help get their endorphins going and calm them down.

"He was supposed to be home in a little bit. But another surgeon got sick, so Daddy has to stay at the hospital and take her shift this evening."

"I don't care!" Jessalyn crossed her arms sulkily. "I. Want. My. Daddy. Now."

Feeling a little overtired and overwrought herself, Merri turned to Jessalyn and assisted her into her jacket. "Well, unfortunately, that is not going to happen."

"Why not?" the twins chorused in perfect unison.

Merri sighed and gave up trying to explain. Hands on their shoulders, she ushered both out the door and onto the front porch. "Because it just isn't." She held their hands as they climbed down the steps. The fresh air and cold winter sunshine had to help. "You two wait right here while I get your tricycles out of the garage." Merri punched in the code and watched as the electric door rose.

By the time she had stepped inside, grabbed the bikes and walked back out, Jeffrey was no longer where he was supposed to be.

Jessalyn, meanwhile, had sunk down on the driveway and was pulling at the Velcro strap of her athletic shoe. "Mommy!" she whined. "Fix this!"

Merri set the bikes down. "What's wrong with it?" She scanned the area for Jeffrey and found him, to her utter dismay, climbing on the stacked firewood, a short distance from the house.

"Oh, my…Jeffrey! Get down from there right now!"

He glared at her with all the pugnacity a four-and-a-half-year-old could muster. Merri knew he was testing her. On days like this, it seemed as if all the twins did was test their limits in one way or another. "I mean it, Jeffrey. You could get hurt!"

Jessalyn continued to wail indignantly, demanding her share of attention, too. "Mommy! My shoe!"

Who said Christmas was a happy time? Merri wondered irritably as she started toward Jeffrey. "I'm counting." If she made it to three, there would be a time-out. A fact her son very well knew.

He picked up a splintery piece of kindling and threw it to the ground as hard as he could.

"One." Merri kept going. Jessalyn kept screaming. Jeffrey threw another piece of wood.

"Two." Merri picked up speed. Another stick went flying, this one so heavy that throwing it nearly rocked Jeffrey off his feet. Merri rushed forward. "That's it, then. Thr—"

She had to dodge hard to avoid another as the last piece of split firewood came tumbling toward her.

Jeffrey screamed again. This time not in rage, but in pain.

THIRTY MINUTES LATER, with the cacophony in the car still at earsplitting levels, Merri was nearly at the hospital. "Jeffrey, Jessalyn, please calm down. It is *just a splinter.*"

"It hurts!" Jeffrey wailed. Beside him, Jessalyn sobbed in sympathy.

Merri knew this was not exactly life or death. She also knew there was no way she was going to be able to get the offending piece of wood out on her own. So here they were, about to make an hysterical entrance into the E.R. that no one would soon forget.

Merri could only imagine what Priscilla Roy would make of this calamity, if and when the esteemed judge heard about it, which she most surely would. Merri eased into a parking space reserved for patients, and cut the motor. She turned to face the twins. "Listen to me," she said in her most stern but soothing voice. "We are going to go in the hospital and—"

"See our daddy!" Jessalyn stopped crying momentarily.

Merri hoped they would. But wary of making another promise that might not come true, especially if Chase was currently in surgery, she said, "We're going to get one of the nurses or the doctors to help us fix Jeffrey's hand. But to do that, we first have got to be quiet, because there are sick people in there. And we don't want to hurt their ears with all this crying."

Amazingly enough—maybe because they had exhausted themselves on the thirty-minute drive to town—the twins fell silent, nodding in assent. There was nothing Merri could do about their red and tear-swollen faces, however, as she got them out of their car seats and guided them into the E.R.

Brianna, one of the triage nurses, came forward. "Hey, Merri."

When Jeffrey burst into tears, Jessalyn teared up, too—out of sympathy.

"What have we got here?" Brianna asked gently.

"A splinter," Merri said, pointing at Jeffrey's hand, which he promptly clasped against his chest.

Merri asked, "I don't suppose Chase...?"

Brianna shook her head. "He's been in surgery. But I heard—"

The elevator doors opened. A big, handsome man in blue scrubs stepped out.

"Daddy!" Jessalyn shouted in joy.

"Daddy!" Jeffrey wiggled out of Merri's arms and ran toward Chase. "Daddy, I got a splinter!" He burst into fresh tears, and Jessalyn joined in. Both hurled themselves into his arms.

And it was only as Chase picked them both up and cuddled them close that Merri realized what the twins had just said.

"They called you Daddy," Merri said, after the splinter had been taken out with one swift, sure, painless pluck of the tweezers, and the tiny hand disinfected, then wrapped with a Scooby-Doo Band-Aid.

"I know." Chase's smile was as big as all Texas. "I heard." He kissed Merri tenderly. "Who said Christmas doesn't come early?"

She and the kids stayed long enough to have a quick dinner with him in the hospital cafeteria, then headed home. Merri skipped baths and put the kids in their pajamas, then in bed. They were asleep before their heads hit the pillow.

The next morning, Chase hit the shower as soon as he got home from the hospital, and she gave the twins bubble baths before breakfast. When her turn came, there was once again no hot water.

Chase grinned, looking surprisingly pleased when she told him she was going to wait an hour or so until the tank had filled again.

"Actually, you may have to delay a little longer than that today," he said, rubbing his jaw.

Merri wasn't surprised he wanted to make love. He often took advantage of the time they were alone, when the kids were at preschool. But he didn't kiss her or lead her toward the bedroom.

Instead, he led her toward a front window.

Two utility trucks were rumbling down the driveway to the ranch house. Merri read the writing on one. "You called a plumber?"

"And an electrician. And someone from the gas company." The trucks parked side by side.

She blinked. "Why?"

Chase hugged her close and grinned. "It's time for your next gift."

"SO YOU LIKED THE TANKLESS water heater?" Emily asked the following day, when she dropped by the ranch house for coffee.

Merri eased away from the kitchen table, where the twins were busy painting the wooden trains they had selected as Christmas gifts for their daddy.

"It's great." She walked Emily out to the garage to show her the new appliance mounted against the wall. "You can see how little space it takes up. And there's no limit on how much hot water is available, since it literally makes it on demand before it goes through the pipes. It can supply three different spigots at once, without any disruption in service." She beamed. "Which means we can have the shower going and still be running the dishwasher and the washing machine, and be okay. The best part is that it's energy and cost efficient."

"You are besotted," Emily teased as they walked back into the house.

Merri cast her friend an amused glance over her shoulder. She moved to the stove to put on the teakettle, thinking about how much fun it had been when she and Chase had christened the new water heater the previous afternoon, after the workmen had left, and again this morning, before the twins woke up. "Besotted by a water heater?" she asked innocently.

As at home in Merri's kitchen as her own, Emily got down two mugs. "I was thinking more about the husband who gave it to you."

Was it that evident? Merri brought out a selection of tea-bags and shrugged. "I am still on my honeymoon, as everyone keeps pointing out to me."

"Uh-huh." Emily plucked a peppermint tea out of the mix and ripped open the seal. "Then what is bothering you? Because I could tell the moment I walked in that something was on your mind."

Merri kept her voice low to avoid alerting the twins, who proved daily they couldn't keep a secret. No matter how hard they tried, they always divulged it in about five seconds. "I haven't been able to figure out what to get Chase," she whispered, dropping a blackberry tea bag into her cup. "Christmas isn't even here and he's already given me a diamond ring, a wedding reception and, as you just saw—" Merri wrinkled her nose playfully "—the water heater of my dreams."

Emily's eyes danced. "Maybe he's the one besotted."

They both were, Merri thought. At least sexually. Romantically? Well, that was still up in the air, and would be until—or if—he fell all the way in love with her.

Because if he didn't, they'd be left with a lopsided arrangement, with her caring more about him than he did about her—and Merri had vowed, after her breakup with Pierce, that she would never put herself in that situation again. But she had, and the weird thing was, she loved Chase so very much, she wasn't even all that sure she minded. He made her so darn happy! Every single day. She could live with loving him more than he loved her. But that wasn't the primary problem today.

Sobering, Merri dragged her attention back to her dilemma. "I know this sounds stupid and frivolous, but I'm serious. Christmas Eve is *tomorrow,* and I want to do something extra special for Chase. Yet I'm still coming up blank."

Everything she looked at, everything she considered, seemed just plain wrong. Lifting the whistling kettle off the stove, Merri admitted, "The only thing I have gotten him so far is a framed photo of him and the kids."

Emily glanced at her. "Not one of the two of you?"

Carefully, Merri filled both their mugs. Reluctant to admit she was still trying not to jinx it, she said, "We're waiting for the proofs from the party photographer. Chase wants to use one of those for his office."

Which made sense, of course, since they were both in their wedding finery.

Emily added sugar to her tea. "Have you asked him what he wants?"

"Yes." Merri removed her tea bag and took a sip. "He says the same thing I always say—that I already have everything I want."

And, Merri realized dreamily, for the first time in her life, it was true. Or would be, if Chase would only fall in love with her the way she was falling in love with him.

"Surely you must have some ideas."

Merri savored the peppermint on her tongue. "That's just it. I don't."

Her friend furrowed her brow. "That isn't like you. You always know what to get, in terms of gifts. What's different about this?"

Merri looked over the counter at the twins, who were so engrossed in decorating the train cars, they were oblivious to the adult conversation. "It's our first Christmas as man and wife," she whispered.

Emily waited.

She drew an enervating breath. Might as well get it all out. "I'm afraid I'll disappoint him."

Emily helped herself to one of the spritz cookies on the counter. "And if you do, then what?"

Merri took her friend's elbow and guided her into the formal dining room. "Then people will see it as proof that we aren't as in sync as a couple should be."

"Ah, yes," Emily retorted gravely, "the Thanksgiving sweet potato casserole travesty."

Abruptly, Merri felt as cranky and out of sorts as the kids had before Jeffrey got the splinter. She looked at the beautifully decorated tree, and the elaborate Christmas village, complete with working Lionel train, which Chase and the kids had added to nearly every day.

"It's not funny." She stalked to the mantel, where four stockings, embroidered with their names, had been hung in a row. Abruptly, although she couldn't say why, she felt near tears. "I'm in crisis here."

Emily walked over to comfort her. "I know you are, and for no reason. Chase adores you. You adore him."

Her friend made it all sound so simple. It wasn't. Not when there was biology, and legalities, and the demands of personal honor involved.

Frustration mounting, Merri turned back to Emily and challenged, "Then why can't I think of something that will demonstrate that to Chase, the way he already has to me?" *Why do I continue to feel at such a loss?* She thought she had put any inadequacy in a relationship behind her.

"You'll come up with a great idea." Emily patted her shoulder encouragingly. "As soon as you calm down and take a breath, and summon up the information and ideas you already have in here." She pointed to Merri's head. "And here." She pointed to her heart. "Just have a little hope and faith, and I promise you it will all work out."

Chapter Fourteen

Pleased that she had finally solved the dilemma that had been plaguing her for weeks, Merri walked down Main Street, Chase's Christmas present in hand. Halfway to her SUV, she encountered their attorney, who also appeared to be taking the afternoon off to do a little last-minute shopping.

Liz smiled as the BlackBerry in her pocket began to hum. "I don't have to ask how things are going," she remarked. "You look happier than I've ever seen you."

Merri stepped back to let another pedestrian pass. "Thanks. I am."

Liz shifted the packages in her arms to be able to check the message on the screen. "The impromptu wedding reception the other night was a very smart move, too."

Shock rendered Merri momentarily speechless. "We didn't do it to prove a point."

"I know that." Liz slid her phone back in her pocket. "I get that it was romantic in origin, and something you and Chase wanted to do." Sobering, she went on, "But it was a very good maneuver to let everyone in town see how you and Chase feel about each other." Her voice dropped a notch. "When you add that to what happened in the emergency room the other night—"

Merri looked at her in surprise. "You heard about that, too?" she whispered.

Liz led her into an alley between two historic brick buildings, so they could talk privately. "The kids calling Chase Daddy and launching themselves into his arms? Yeah. I heard about it. At least a dozen times, if not more. Apparently, there wasn't a dry eye in the house."

Merri gulped, feeling a wave of emotion. Talk about joy and newfound love! This sure was the season... "It was pretty touching," she admitted, trying not to become teary.

Liz's expression gentled. "My point is, when we talked ten days ago, you and Chase were worried about the public perception of your marriage, and the fact the kids didn't seem to be accepting him. Now, thanks to recent events—some scripted, some not—word on the street is that has changed. So much that the four of you could be the poster happy family."

Merri couldn't help but feel pleased about that, especially given the inept start she and Chase had experienced, trying to acclimate to each other and orient the kids to all the sudden changes.

She breathed in the yuletide fragrance of freshly baked gingerbread cookies from the bakery two doors down. "You think it will get back to Judge Roy?"

"Please!" Liz silenced her phone when it went off again. "In a community as close-knit as this? Of course it will."

Relief flowed through Merri. It certainly would help to replace the initial impressions she and Chase and the kids had made with something a lot more positive.

"I still can't guarantee results," Liz reminded her. "No attorney can do that. But thanks to recent events, your chances for the outcome you want are a whole lot better than they were initially. So..." She grinned. "...merry Christmas!"

Merri beamed. "Merry Christmas to you, too!"

"WHAT'S GOT YOU FEELING so chipper?" Chase asked Merri after they had put the kids in bed that evening.

Happy to finally have a moment alone with her husband, Merri told him about her conversation with Liz.

Chase didn't look as surprised as she had been. "I was hoping that would help," he murmured, following her into the laundry room.

A shimmer of unease slid down Merri's spine. She paused in front of the clothes dryer. "That wasn't why you threw the party and gave me the diamond ring, was it?" she asked in a soft, wary tone. "To make our marriage seem more legitimate, and therefore help us in court?"

If that was the case, it took all the joy out of both events. It also made her a romantic fool, because she'd thought—hoped—that his actions had been motivated by their new-found passion and growing feelings for each other.

He reassured her with a sober glance. "No. Of course not. I gave you the ring and the party because our new bond deserves to be celebrated. I'm honored that you agreed to share your life with me and be my wife, and I want everyone to know how much you mean to me."

Merri wanted to shout out her love to the whole world, too. The only problem was, Chase had never mentioned love. Or even infatuation.

She studied him, knowing him well enough to realize there was more there, just beneath the surface. "And yet you're not unhappy it's apparently had this result, are you?"

He shrugged. "I want this matter settled as soon as possible, Merri. I want us to be a complete family, the two of us co-guardians of the kids." He put his hands on her shoulders and intimately searched her face. "I thought that was what you wanted, too."

"Of course it is," she declared hotly, wondering how they had taken something happy and turned it into conflict. Tomorrow was Christmas Eve. She didn't want to argue with Chase.

His hands slid down her arms to her wrists. "Then?"

She leaned back against the washer and forced herself to go on. "It occurs to me now that this could backfire. Particularly if Judge Roy were to perceive it as an attempt by us to put something over on the court." The woman had certainly warned them...

Chase settled next to Merri. His back to the dryer, he laced a protective arm about her shoulders, drawing her in close to his side. "I don't think she will take that view. I think at the end of the day she'll know we're sincere."

Merri hoped Chase wasn't just telling her what he thought she wanted to hear. She resisted the urge to rest her cheek against his shoulder, and forced herself to play the part of devil's advocate. "And if Judge Roy doesn't?" *What then?*

Chase intwined their fingers, squeezed. His gaze never left her face. "Then we keep on trying, because you and I know the truth. That our intentions have always been honorable." He brushed a strand of hair from her cheek, and his low voice was as soothing as his touch. "Everything we've done here has been to protect the kids and build a strong and loving family for them." He paused to let his words sink in. "And as Kate pointed out to us, our relationship with each other is the foundation for that."

Which meant they had to be fully married, so if asked, they could swear under oath that theirs was a real marriage in every way.

Chase misunderstood the reason behind her anxiety. "I know there's still a lot up in the air, Merri, but it's all going to work out for us. You'll see."

MERRI SPENT THE NIGHT IN Chase's arms and woke up feeling much better. It was silly to worry about things they had no control of in the end. What mattered now was the twins' first Christmas with a mommy and a daddy.

As if to drive home that fact, the first thing Merri saw that morning when she opened up her email was an electronic holiday card for the entire family.

"Look, Mommy," Jessalyn cried excitedly when Merri showed the photo greeting to the twins. "It's Addie and Nissa and Davita and Harmony and Polly and Starr!"

All were wearing their Santa hats again. All were holding signs naming their various hometowns, with the message, "Next Stop, Christmas!" beneath.

Chase, who was manning the griddle, making pancakes, came over to see, too. He grinned at the holiday gretting.

"What's that?" Jeffrey asked, pointing to a digital clock sign that said 84:22.

"I think it's how much time is left before they have to catch their flight overseas, to go back to work in the field hospital."

"Sorry you're not going?" The words slipped out before Merri could stop herself.

Chase held her eyes and shook his head. "I'm right where I'm supposed to be." He gazed at her contentedly, then reeled her in and kissed her soundly.

"Ooh" the twins said in unison. "You're kissing!"

They sure were, Merri thought, her spirits rising and her knees wobbling. It was times like this, when he was holding her in his arms, that it felt as if the barriers around their hearts had completely fallen away. She reveled in the feeling of hard male muscle pressed up against her, and the longing she saw in his eyes.

Fortunately, the kids had already moved on. "Does Santa Claus kiss anybody?" Jessalyn asked, propping her hand on her chin. She watched as Chase went back to the griddle to flip the pancakes, which were a perfect golden-brown.

Jeffrey traced the label on the syrup bottle already on the table. He scowled thoughtfully. "Maybe his reindeer," he suggested finally.

Merri grinned at the mental image. "And Mrs. Claus," she said.

Chase carried two plates of silver-dollar pancakes to the table and set them in front of the kids. "Speaking of Santa—" he flashed Merri a look, then returned to the griddle "—is there anything you little ones forgot to tell him that you want?"

Jeffrey and Jessalyn looked at each other and seemed to communicate without saying a word. "No," they said finally, in unison.

"You sure?" Merri asked.

"He knows. We already told him. At the hospital Christmas party, remember?" Jessalyn stated.

But whatever they'd said remained a mystery to their parents. "You can always tell us, too," Merri said.

"No, we can't," Jeffrey argued stubbornly. "You can't tell anyone your wish or it won't come true. Remember what you said when we blew out the candles on our cake?"

The logic of a four-and-a-half-year-old! "I think that's just birthday wishes," Merri told him, adding butter and syrup to both stacks.

"Nuh-uh! All wishes are secret," Jessalyn declared, "if you want them to come true." She and Jeffrey stared into each other's eyes yet again, in that magical way they had. "And we really really do."

"You can't tell anyone but Santa what you want for Christmas, and we already did," Jeffrey explained.

Merri looked at Chase. He looked at her. This was not the kind of thing they were going to be able to reason with the kids about.

So they did the only thing they could do, and called

Dylan, who'd played Santa, when the twins were out of earshot.

"Trust me," Dylan reiterated, "it's the kind of thing you'd much rather hear from them. I'm sure they'll tell you tomorrow, when they wake up and get what they've been wanting for weeks now." He exhaled sharply. "You *are* going to be off, aren't you, Chase? You wouldn't miss this?"

"I've got today and tomorrow off," he assured him. The other surgeons in rotation, who didn't have small children anymore, had seen to that.

"Well, then," Dylan said mysteriously before hanging up the phone, "you're all set."

TEN HOURS LATER, THE KIDS were finally asleep. The cookies and milk they'd set out for "Santa" had been consumed, the presents arranged beneath the tree. Blissfully, Chase and Merri settled down for some quiet time in front of the fire.

Chase's eyes sparkled. "Was that home pregnancy test kit in the bathroom yours?"

Aware this was the most exciting Christmas Eve she'd ever had, and that Christmas Day promised to be better yet, Merri flushed. She tucked her hand in his larger, callused palm. "You weren't supposed to see that!"

His heated gaze trailed over her features before returning with slow deliberation to her eyes. "I probably wouldn't have, if I hadn't been looking for a new blade for my razor." He paused, his expression becoming even more hopeful and intent. "Are you pregnant?"

Glad she had him beside her, Merri gripped his hand all the tighter. "I don't know yet. I'm not supposed to take the test until I'm at least a week late, and that won't be until the twenty-seventh." Three days from now…

Tenderly, he kissed the back of her hand. "But you think there's a good chance."

She looked deep into his eyes. "Usually, I'm like clock-work, and this cycle I'm not."

He grinned like a proud papa-to-be. "Well, then, congratulations." He shifted her onto his lap and delivered a long, sexy kiss.

She leaned back, appreciating the excited gleam in his eyes, knowing what a great daddy he already was, and would be to another child, too. "Congratulations to you, too," she replied softly. "But let's not tempt fate by talking about it too much." It scared her to want something—or someone—this much. And she did want Chase, so very much.

He hugged her close. "Agreed. We'll have plenty of time for that later. In the meantime," he murmured, drawing back to look into her eyes once again, "since I think we might be just a little busy tomorrow morning, making Christmas dinner and setting up the new set of train tracks, I'd like to give you your last gift this evening, if that's okay."

Merri bounded off his lap. "More than okay." She turned around with a wink and a curtsy. "Since I've got something for you, too."

Moments later, they settled on the floor in front of the beautifully lit and decorated tree, presents on their laps. "Ladies first," he said, smiling.

Achingly aware of just how much she had come to depend on him, Merri opened with trembling fingers the gift box he handed her. Inside was a platinum charm necklace, with the birthstones of all four of them set inside intricately intertwined hearts. He couldn't have picked a more meaningful present. Aware he'd come close to her heart, as always, Merri sighed with pleasure. "Oh, Chase. It's gorgeous! Thank you!"

She paused to kiss him, reveling in the minty taste of him, then handed him a long, slender box that contained the gift she had spent so much time picking out. She beamed at him, hoping he would like his present as much as she liked hers. "Your turn."

He waggled his eyebrows teasingly, then tore open the wrapping. Inside was a thick envelope bearing the local travel agency's logo. Curiosity piqued, he turned back the flap and saw the itinerary. A grin as big as Texas spread across his rugged features. "A cross-country train trip to Disneyland!"

Eager for him to see, Merri pointed out the rest. "And a plane flight back." She'd attended to every detail of the dream vacation. "It'll be the twins' first time on a train and a plane and at Disneyland. And their first big family vacation, too."

Chase laughed in delight. "They're going to love it. I love it." He gathered her close in a hug, then drew back, looking handsome and at ease in the soft twinkling lights of the tree. "Thank you." He paused to look deep into her eyes. "This is an incredible gift."

"I'm glad you like it," Merri said softly. Glad she understood what was in his heart, as surely as he did hers.

Contentedly, they lingered before the fire, enjoying each other's company, then went upstairs to further celebrate their first Christmas together. Feeling the connection between them deepening, they made tender, exquisite love, and Merri fell asleep wrapped in Chase's arms, dreaming of the baby she was sure they had made.

They woke at just past five the next morning. Jessalyn and Jeffrey were standing beside their bed, the two preschoolers jumping up and down with glee.

"Mommy! Daddy! Is it time yet?" Jeffrey tugged on Chase's arm.

Jessalyn tugged on Merri's. "Can we go downstairs? And see if Santa came?"

Chuckling, Chase and Merri sat up, and rubbed the sleep from their eyes. "Absolutely," Chase said in his gravelly voice. Grinning, the four of them clasped hands and went downstairs.

The tree with all its colored lights sparkled in the semi-darkness. At the sight of the presents beneath it, the kids let out whoops of delight. Mad, happy chaos followed. Gifts were opened, one after another, and exclaimed over. Pleased that she and Chase had done well in selecting presents for the twins, because all she really wanted was for them to be happy, especially today, Merri smiled at them affectionately.

"So, did you get everything you wanted?" Chase asked finally, still curious about their secret request to Dylan Reeves, aka Santa Claus. "Everything you asked Santa for?"

"Of course." The twins looked at Chase and smiled even more mysteriously. Then they went back to examining their new trains.

Merri and Chase exchanged baffled glances. "You want to tell us what it was?" Merri asked, as she helped to take a new doll baby out of its box.

The twins shrugged, as if the answer was obvious. They dropped what they were doing and ambled over to Chase. "For Daddy to still be here and not go away," Jessalyn said. "And see?" She pointed at him for proof. "He's right here. Just like we asked Santa."

Dumbfounded, Merri and Chase stared at each other. No wonder Dylan hadn't wanted to divulge their wish.

Chase gathered the kids onto his lap, then took Merri's hand and reeled her in close, too, so they were all sitting on the sofa, snuggling together. Gently he smoothed a hand down the twins' spines, and asked, "Why would you think I was leaving?"

Beginning to look a little worried, Jessalyn confided, "Because all the grown-ups said so."

"When?" Merri asked in alarm.

The little girl frowned. "At the welcome-home party. Everyone talked about how long you were gone away, Daddy, and how they never figured you'd stay in Laramie County, if you ever came home again."

To her distress, Merri remembered something like that being said. Countless times. She should have known the precocious, ultra-observant duo would pick up on it and internalize it.

Jeffrey leaned forward to confide, "The army ladies were sad you were leaving *them,* too. Especially Miss Starr. But Miss Addie and Miss Harmony said *they* weren't surprised. They always knew you'd go back to Texas someday and that you had to leave them, whether any of them liked it or not!"

"We didn't want you to leave *us,* too," Jessalyn allowed defiantly, tears of anguish beginning to shimmer in her eyes.

"Yeah! 'Cause—" Jeffrey hiccupped and wrapped his arms around Chase's neck "—we like having you around."

"And we love you, Daddy," they finished in unison.

Cuddling them close, Chase said thickly, "I love you both, too."

"So you won't ever leave us?" Jeffrey asked, while Merri swallowed around the lump in her throat.

"I won't ever leave you," he promised the kids gently, kissing them on the tops of their heads. Grinning, he ruffled their hair. "So we don't need to worry about that, okay?"

They beamed, the last traces of sadness leaving their faces. "Okay." They hugged Chase one more time, then raced off to play with their toys again.

"That was some Christmas present you just got," Merri told Chase, still feeling a little choked up by the revelation of just how much they adored their new daddy. They'd come to count on him almost as much as she did!

He nodded, then gave her a steady look that set her pulse

pounding. "It sure was." He drew her close and kissed her, his hand drifting to her tummy, hovering protectively over the baby that just might be inside her.

"And the best thing, Merri," he whispered, "is that for us, this is just the beginning."

THE DAY AFTER CHRISTMAS, Merri woke before dawn. Still so happy over the way the holiday had gone, she expected to be bursting with energy. Instead, she felt achy and out of sorts. Attributing it to all the activity of the past few days, she shook off her lethargy.

Chase studied her sluggish movements with concern. "You sure you don't want me to do the milking?" he asked gently, getting up, too.

Merri appreciated his offer, even as she refused with a shake of her head. The dairy farming was her thing; she wasn't about to push it off on him.

"It's my responsibility." Because Slim had come in on Christmas Eve and Christmas Day, she was handling both morning and evening chores for the next several days.

She sauntered toward him, loving the way he looked in low-slung pajama pants and a day's growth of beard, and she ran a palm over his warm, bare chest. "And you have to work this evening."

He kissed her as if rest was the last thing on his mind, then promised, "I'll have breakfast ready for you when you come back in." He kissed her one more time before heading downstairs.

Merri went into the bathroom to get dressed and to her dismay, quickly realized why she felt so icky.

Chase knew something was up the moment he saw her face. He stopped filling her stainless-steel thermos and put the coffee decanter back on the warmer. "What's wrong?" he asked gruffly.

Regret at having spoken too eagerly, too soon, filled her cheeks with heat. "I'm not pregnant," Merri admitted with embarrassment.

His face fell, and somehow it helped to know that he was disappointed, too. He came toward her, arms outstretched, and held her tightly. "Ah, Merri, I'm sorry."

His tenderness melting her heart all the more, Merri fought back a sudden rush of tears. "I'm the one who's sorry," she said, hoarse with disappointment. How could she have been so foolish? So hopeful? Knowing what the odds were that she would conceive during the first menstrual cycle of trying, whether they'd known when she was ovulating or not?

Merri gulped. "I—"

"Hey. Hush…" Chase stroked a hand down her back, then hugged her again. "You're going to get pregnant." His deep voice rumbled in her ear. "Probably sooner than you think." He drew back and, hooking his thumbs beneath her chin, lifted her face to his. Grinned in the familiar, unrepentant bad-boy way he employed whenever he wanted to make wild, passionate love with her. "In the meantime," he murmured with a wicked gleam in his eyes, "think of all the fun we're going to have trying."

He was ready now. Feeling his erection pressed against her, Merri ran her palms down his back to his buttocks. "You're such a great guy." She fitted her lower half to his, knowing another bout of lovemaking would make them both feel better.

But right now, the herd was waiting….

She rose on tiptoe and kissed the underside of his jaw. "Rain check?"

"An extra special rain check. Whenever you feel up to it," he promised huskily. "Until then… my offer to do the milking this morning is still good."

"No." Knowing she needed the time to herself, to think about—and accept—the disappointment not being pregnant had brought, she channeled her inner sassiness. "But I look forward to that breakfast you're going to fix me when I return."

Chase grinned and promised, "I'll make sure it's an extra special one, too." They kissed again, and he swatted her playfully. "Hurry back."

So glad he was in her life, Merri dutifully agreed.

Unfortunately, when she returned to the ranch house, she quickly realized their first holiday together had taken another unplanned turn.

A rental car with out-of-state license plates sat in the driveway, a lone suitcase and Santa hat in the backseat, a single coffee cup in the holder. Unexpected company? Again?

Merri had a sinking feeling she knew exactly who it was.

Chapter Fifteen

Chase stared at Starr, glad that the twins were still up-stairs, sound asleep, and that Merri was out in the barn. The last thing she needed was to find him with a woman hell-bent on making a pass at him. "You have to leave," he told Starr grimly.

She ignored his attempts to politely show her to the door, and stalked past him to the kitchen. "Not until I save you from yourself."

This, Chase thought, did not sound good. He tried to head her off. "We've been friends a long time." Which was the only reason he was being as circumspect as he was.

Moisture brimmed in the young nurse's eyes. "And I've loved you forever," she said thickly.

"I'm sorry, Starr." Everyone had hinted that this was the case. He had figured he could avert confrontation by pre-tending not to notice his former coworker's crush. As firmly and kindly as possible, he said, "I don't feel that way about you. I never have. I never will."

Tears spilled down her face. "You don't know what you feel! If you did, you never would have married Merri after being back in Texas for just a few days!"

There was a certain truth to that observation, Chase ad-mitted ruefully to himself. When he'd first become involved with Merri, he'd had no idea how hard and fast he would fall, or how mind-blowingly happy she—and the kids—would make him. But now he did have a family, and he was determined to protect them.

He sent Starr a warning glance. "You don't know anything about that."

The nurse scoffed and stomped closer. "I know this. You haven't let yourself be serious about anyone since your engagement ended."

Chase shrugged. Nothing complicated about that. "I didn't want to date."

Starr glared at him. "And now suddenly, out of the blue, you want to marry someone—*just like that?* Be honest." She balled her hands in frustration. "This is all about honor. You're with Merri out of some cockeyed notion of responsibility for your brother's kids."

It had started out that way. Now? "It's complicated," Chase finally allowed. About so much more than just the twins and his inability to legally claim them as his own without defaming the Armstrong family name. "I don't expect you to understand," he said grimly. Nor would anyone else. Chase knew he was doing what was best for everyone.

Starr paced back and forth, years of emotion spilling out. "I understand this. You can't build happiness out of a need to behave with integrity."

He'd done pretty well so far. Because the truth was, the past five weeks with Merri and the kids had been the happiest of his life.

"Standing by family and behaving honorably will take you only so far. If anything, your work in the field hospital should have shown you how short and precious our lives are! You have to stop worrying about everyone else and start seeing to your own needs." Starr grabbed a tissue and wiped the moisture from her cheeks. "You're such a good guy, Chase…" She held out her hands beseechingly. "You deserve so much more than a dutiful marriage to Merri can give you."

"It's true," a familiar voice said from the doorway.

Swearing inwardly, Chase turned to find his wife standing there, ashen-faced, regarding him with icy eyes.

Merri continued into the kitchen, stepping carefully. "Chase is a great guy." She looked at Starr and continued in a low, flat tone, "He deserves everything life has to offer. We all do."

"Which is why—" Chase said firmly, taking Starr by the arm "—you are leaving." He marched their uninvited guest through the foyer. "I wish you all the best. I really do." He opened the door wide and guided her onto the porch, his expression stern. "It's not here. It's not with me. And it never will be."

Starr dug in her heels and glared back at Merri. "I don't know what this hold is that you have on him, but if you have any heart at all, you'll let him go, because you're never going to make him happy. Duty isn't the same as love." Tear streamed from her eyes. "I get that you need a man to help you bring up the twins, but it doesn't have to be him."

Actually, Chase thought, given that they were his, it kind of did.

"And it doesn't mean he has to marry you!" Starr spat out.

Chase caught the door with his hand before she could slam it shut. He closed it quietly, so as not to wake the children still sleeping upstairs.

As always, when returning from working in the dairy barn, Merri appeared to want nothing more than a hot shower and a set of clean clothes. She walked back through the hall to the kitchen, set her thermos on the counter.

"I'm sorry that happened," Chase said, eyeing her pink cheeks and pale lips. "Sorry you had to hear that."

Merri's shoulders slumped in defeat. "I'm not. Because Starr's right." She gazed at him, her expression twisted with remorse. "We shouldn't be together. Not like this. Not for the long haul."

"THERE'S EVEN A TERM FOR IT," Merri murmured wearily, reflecting on the conversation she'd had with Addie weeks before. "Crisis bonding."

"There's no question that the situation we have found ourselves in with the kids did turn both our lives upside down."

"No kidding." She'd been so full of guilt about not going to Chase sooner with what she knew—and so fearful about what the emotional fallout would be—that she'd allowed herself to think only in the short-term.

"We did the right thing, Merri, getting married."

Had they? "I thought so at the time."

Looking back, she wondered how she could have been so reckless. Letting herself believe that everything would work out the way she wanted, over time.

That Chase could give the kids the security and love they deserved, and her the baby she wanted. And then, when one thing led to another, and their blinding passion seduced her into letting her guard down further, she had convinced herself that their marriage could be real and lasting because her love was strong enough for both of them.

Never thinking about how much she was taking from him.

Now she knew better.

Because now she understood what it was like to love someone completely. The problem was, Chase didn't feel that way about her.

To not have that—ever—because you were tied to someone else out of duty or obligation was just plain wrong. Starr was right about that.

Chase edged closer. "And now you think our marriage was a mistake."

"For the long haul? Yes. It was."

His jaw set. "How can you say that?"

Tears welled in her eyes, but Merri stayed strong. "Because it's true," she said quietly, wishing with all her heart that it wasn't. "We're through the bulk of the crisis now. The twins have accepted you as their daddy in a way that will never be undone."

His lips formed a sober downward curve. "So you're dumping me."

"Suggesting we take a step back now, while we still can, and reevaluate. Because Starr is right to be concerned, even if she doesn't know all the details behind our marriage."

"Like the fact I want you and you want me…and that's not going to change, no matter what label you put on it?"

He was talking about the purely physical again. "That particular turn in our relationship was born out of extreme stress and pressure to do the right thing by you and the kids. Our desire for each other was fueled by all the emotion and potential heartache we were facing. And those are factors no one else but us can ever possibly understand, because they didn't live through this the way we have."

"It seems to me that's all the more reason we should stay together," he argued.

If only he had said he loved her, or could love her…

"Because we're bound to get closer, over time."

"Or grow apart, as people sometimes do, once the crisis that brought them together ends," she countered.

Chase studied her, legs braced apart, hands on his waist. "This is because you found out you aren't pregnant, isn't it?"

Merri flushed under his steady regard. "That has nothing to do with it."

"Really?" He released a short breath and came even closer. "If the situation was reversed, if you were pregnant right now, would you be standing here, telling me we made a mistake and needed to end this?"

Misery engulfed her anew. "The point is I'm not pregnant." And that was a good thing. Wasn't it?

He turned a disillusioned glance her way, his hurt and dismay evident. "And you won't give me a chance to remedy that."

Merri hurt, too, but she knew the pain they felt now was only a fraction of what they would feel if they continued recklessly down this path. "You deserve love, Chase. I do, too."

He recoiled as if she had slapped him. "Or in other words," he said bitterly, "just like my ex, the minute things don't go your way, you're out of here. There is no compromise. No meeting each other halfway. No putting each other's needs and desires, dreams and goals, above our own."

He didn't know how much Merri wanted to forget being noble, forget doing the honorable thing, and welcome him back into her arms and her bed. She swallowed hard, forcing herself to go on. "You heard what Kate said. To have a successful family, we need a strong and loving relationship, as foundation." *Love* being the operative word.

He braced himself as if for battle. "We have that."

Merri shook her head sadly. "Not in the way she meant. We need to be soul mates, just like every other happily married couple we know. Like Paige and Kurt. Emily and Dylan. And we're not, Chase." She cut him off with a lift of her hand. "Given how we rushed into this, there's no way we could be."

"I disagree. Sure, the beginning was a little rocky, but lately it's been great."

She held her head high. They had managed to become effective co-parents and even friends with benefits. "But what happens if you do fall in love with someone else one day?" she challenged, her heart breaking at the thought. *What then?*

"I told you. I don't feel that way about Starr."

"But you might feel that way about some woman eventually, Chase." *You certainly haven't intimated you feel that way about me.*

He reached for her tenderly. "I have everything I need with you."

Except love, Merri thought. And love was what he needed most of all. Splaying her hand across his chest, she pushed him away, determined to do what was right. "Look. We'll figure this out. We'll find a way to go forward as co-guardians of the kids."

"And until then?" he asked, his resentment obvious.

Disappointment stabbed her heart, even as she forced herself to be practical. "We disrupt the twins' lives as little as possible, and go back to the way it was when you first moved in with us."

His expression closed. "Separate bedrooms."

Merri nodded, her heart now officially broken. "And a marital relationship that is anchored by friendship, nothing more."

CHASE PAUSED IN THE DOORWAY of Kate Marten's office. "Got a minute?"

The grief counselor stood and motioned him in, then shut the door for privacy. "What's on your mind?"

Chase had never been the kind of guy who went to others for advice on his personal life. It was what it was. He dealt with his problems on his own. But this was different. It wasn't just him. Or Merri. Regardless of what had happened in their marriage, they still had to protect the kids. And right now, he had no idea how to do that.

"When I first came back, and Merri and I got married, you thought it might be some sort of stress reaction to being back home, after years doing trauma surgeries in a military field hospital."

Kate interrupted with a lift of her hand. "Obviously, I was wrong about that."

"Actually, your instincts were right on. There were extenuating circumstances behind our rush to the altar."

Kate looked at him curiously.

"And as you guessed, some things I do need to talk about." *With someone I can trust to give me rock-solid advice.* "So if I ask for doctor-patient confidentiality—"

"You've got it," Kate promised. "What you say here will go no farther than this office."

Relieved to be able to speak to someone with perspective, Chase took a seat on the sofa. While she listened, occasionally taking notes, he told her about the deception his late brother and sister-in-law had perpetuated, and the necessary decisions that had followed.

"So it was a marriage of convenience."

Chase nodded, realizing now how unromantic that sounded. "It started out that way."

"And then changed into something much more viable."

His gut knotted. Had he ever been what Merri needed? Wanted? "I thought it had."

Kate smiled sympathetically. "So did everyone else."

Chase slumped back on the sofa. "Apparently everyone—including me—was wrong." He scrubbed a hand over his face and scowled. "Merri told me yesterday that she doesn't think we should continue trying to make our marriage a real union. She wants a more platonic arrangement."

Kate pursed her lips. "And you agreed."

Slowly, Chase released a breath. "I made a commitment to be a father to the twins. To provide the most normal, loving environment possible for them."

She nodded in approval. "And you're keeping that promise."

"Yes." Even though he'd had the faith and hope kicked out of him, it was the only honorable way to proceed.

Kate gave him a long, probing look. "Can you do that?"

Chase paused, giving the question the consideration it deserved. "Technically, yes. Merri and I have enough willpower to adhere to whatever restrictions we agree upon." At least in terms of their physical relationship. Emotionally, well, his feelings were going to be a lot harder to corral. Especially when it came to putting her back in the friend category, and nothing more.

Kate tapped her pen on her notepad. "Then what's the problem?"

For starters? "The kids. They're pretty sensitive to what goes on around them." Chase explained the twins' wish that he still be there on Christmas Day.

"You think if you and Merri are no longer intimate the twins will figure out something is amiss?"

"Given what they've already been able to observe and surmise? I know they will." Chase leaned forward, hands clasped between his knees. "And the thing is, I don't want them hurt." And because he was selfish....

"I don't want to give them up," he admitted. "I've already missed almost five years of their lives." The thought of losing even more time with them was unbearable. "I don't want to turn into a three-days-a-week, every-other-holiday dad." Which was the kind of arrangement an eventual divorce would bring.

"And that's why you're determined to stay married to Merri."

"Yes," he said gruffly. Even though the thought of never being *with* her again—after all that spectacular lovemaking they'd shared—was like having his heart crushed in a vise. There wasn't going to be a part of him that didn't miss her desperately.

"Hmm."

"What?" Chase demanded when the counselor said nothing more.

Kate lifted an eyebrow. "I think you might want to ask yourself why the two of you are still so amenable to the idea of living under the same roof—when there are so many other options available."

"IS THERE ANY WAY TO DELAY the hearing with Judge Roy without jeopardizing Chase's request for co-guardianship?" Merri asked their attorney early the following day. Another night sleeping down the hall from Chase had left her restless and upset. Worse, despite her Oscar-worthy performance at breakfast, the kids were beginning to pick up on it. Chase had noticed, too.

Liz ushered her into the conference room.

"Why would we want to request that? What's going on?"

Merri swallowed, feeling abruptly near tears. Why had she allowed herself to be so reckless and make such a mess of things? Especially when she knew better than to take anything on faith! "I made a mistake, marrying Chase."

Liz patted her shoulder. "And you came to that conclusion because…?"

Her guilt intensifying, Merri slumped into a chair. "He deserves to love and be loved…."

"Isn't that what's been going on with the two of you?" the lawyer asked.

Merri pushed aside the memory of the hurt and confusion in Chase's eyes when she'd told him their physical relationship was over. "Maybe for me," she allowed softly, realizing how different life would be if her feelings were returned.

"Not for him."

Merri shrugged. "He does love the kids with all his heart. And they love him, too, so very much."

"What do you think he feels for you?"

Did she even want to answer that?

Liz pressed on. "Pretend we're under oath here. Pretend I'm Judge Roy. Answer the question. What do you think he feels for you?"

Realizing their attorney was only doing her job, Merri forced herself to reply. "I think Chase feels lust for me." There was no doubt their passion was incredible. "And friendship." To the point he made her feel she could talk to him about practically anything. Except anything that would put him on the spot and make them both uncomfortable. "And a close bond because we both share a biological connection to the kids, and want to parent them."

Liz sat back in her chair, a bemused look on her face.

"What are you thinking?" Merri asked impatiently.

She flashed a wry smile. "How ironic it is that just when all the speculation has completely died down, and everyone believes that you and Chase and the kids absolutely belong together, the two of you want out."

"I didn't say we wanted this."

"Of course not," Liz murmured, unconvinced.

Merri threw up her hands in frustration. "But it's the only sensible way to proceed. Naively, I had hoped otherwise, but let's get real—Chase and I are not going to be happy staying under the same roof if we are not sleeping together as man and wife."

"Of course not."

"That kind of proximity... well, you've seen Chase. You know how incredibly handsome he is." In bed. And out. The truth was, all he had to do was breathe and...

"And he thinks you're easy on the eyes, too, I gather?" they lawyer aked dryly.

Merri frowned. "I'm being serious here, Liz."

Her attorney's eyes gleamed. "I can see that."

Merri drew a breath and forced herself to go on, even more frankly, "Anyway, I was thinking that maybe if we delayed, we could use the time to figure out a way to convince Judge Roy and the court to allow Chase to live on the property—perhaps in a separate dwelling—and continue to be a dad to the kids."

"As a co-guardian?"

"Yes. Since he loves the twins and they love him. So they wouldn't lose any time with each other, the way people do in a normal divorce or legal separation."

"And you'd be okay with that?"

"I'm okay with anything that makes him and the kids happy."

And keeps him a safe distance away. So that my constant lusting after him won't be an issue for either of us.

Liz played with her pen. "What does Chase think about this?"

"I haven't spoken to him yet. I wanted to make sure it would work, that his rights were protected, before proceeding."

The attorney set down her pen and speculated for a moment in silence. "I see," she said finally.

"You look like you do," Merri allowed nervously, "and you don't." Was her blunt honesty about to get them in even more trouble? It felt as if their lives were already screwed up enough.

"Maybe because you're acting like you care more about Chase's needs than your own. Which, I have to tell you, is not usually the case in proposed divorce action. And I have to ask you, Merri." Liz paused to give her a long, searching glance. "Why is that?"

MERRI THOUGHT FOR THE REST of the day about what Liz had asked her.

By evening, she knew what she had to do. But Chase was at the hospital and not due home until noon the following day. Which was okay. It gave Merri time to arrange for the kids to be elsewhere, and figure out what she was going to say.

Unfortunately, Chase didn't walk in at twelve-thirty, as scheduled. Nor was he there at one o'clock, or two.

Her spirits sinking, Merri was just reaching for the cord to unplug the Christmas tree lights when she heard the front door open and close.

Her heart racing with anticipation, she straightened.

Chase strode in.

He looked as tired as she would have expected after an eighteen hour-plus shift.

He was also freshly showered, shaved, wearing a neatly pressed shirt and slacks. Looking more ready for a date than bed, he shrugged out of his coat, dropped it on the arm of the chair and kept right on coming toward her. He pulled her into his arms and pressed his body against hers, his mouth against her hair.

It was the kind of casual, wordless greeting two long-time lovers gave each other, and despite herself, she melted into him.

He felt so damn good. So warm and strong and male.

Beneath his shirt, she could feel the beating of his heart. Briefly, Merri closed her eyes, breathing in the tantalizingly familiar fragrance of soap and man. He kissed the top of her head, the gesture casual and tender, then ever so reluctantly released her and stepped back.

Merri tilted her chin and gazed into his eyes. Unbelievably, he looked as if he had missed her as much as she had missed him. And it had only been forty-eight hours since they'd stopped behaving as man and wife. Forty-eight long, lonely, unbearably miserable hours.

"Hey," Merri said softly, joy mingling with the longing deep inside her.

He was here. He was happy to see her. It wasn't the answer to all their problems, but it was a good first step, she realized, as courage flooded her anew.

His gaze drifted over her, as if he was drinking in and memorizing every detail. He reached up and tucked a strand of hair behind her ear, with a look of forgiveness she hadn't expected to see in his eyes. "Where are the kids?" he asked softly.

The lump in her throat was back, as another wave of anxiety slid through her. "Playing with the triplets, at Paige and Kurt's."

Chase covered Merri's hand with his and locked eyes with her. "They're due to be picked up when?"

"Six this evening." Her throat tightened even more, making it difficult to swallow. She consulted her watch. "Which gives us about three and a half hours." *To work things out and find a holiday miracle of our very own, before the New Year.*

Chase's gaze intensified, the silence reinforcing all that was at stake. "Good." He ran a thumb over her knuckles. "'Cause there's a lot I want to say."

Glad she hadn't unplugged the Christmas tree, after all,

since it gave a much needed element of cheer to the wintry stillness of the living room, Merri drew a bolstering breath. Ready to make whatever sacrifices were required, she looked deep into his eyes and said, "Okay."

He gazed down at her with the quiet intensity she loved so much. "I talked to Kate Marten yesterday."

Ignoring the sudden wobbliness of her knees, Merri tried to figure out where all this was going. The same place she wanted, she hoped. Blinking back a mist of emotion, she confided, "I talked to Liz Cartwright."

He came closer. "There's not going to be any divorce." His voice was a sexy rumble. "I won't agree to it."

Merri splayed her hands across his chest. "Okay."

He wrapped his arms around her and held fast. "No more pretending for all the world to be married, either. Because we *are* married, Merri." He tightened his grip on her affectionately. "I don't know how or when it became so much more…" He let the words sink in, then flashed the sexy grin she loved so much. "The realness of it sort of snuck up on me." He lowered his head and kissed her sweetly.

Merri slipped her arms about his neck and kissed him back, then admitted, "It took me by surprise, too."

They shared another kiss, even more ardent and persuasive. "I've been trying not to rush you, but sometimes there's just no slowing down what's in your heart."

"No kidding." Merri laughed shakily, as she realized all her dreams were about to come true. "It's like a freight train, going full speed."

He nodded in agreement, then forged on, the words coming from deep in his soul. "That being the case, you might as well know. I love you, Merri." She let out an exultant laugh, and he soldiered on. "And I'm pretty sure if you really think about it, you'll realize that you love me, too."

His confidence was as contagious as his bravery. "I don't

have to think about it—I know how I feel. I've loved you for some time, Chase Armstrong." Relieved to finally be able to admit what was in her heart, Merri went up on tiptoe and kissed him with every bit of passion and joy she possessed. "I'm head over heels in love with you," she whispered.

He pulled her nearer, still, until they were pressed intimately together. "So no more talk about what we have not being enough."

Merri cuddled close, ready—finally—to open up her heart and take all the risks required. "None."

His gaze was steady and sincere. "It's not just about doing what's right for the kids anymore. It's about doing what is right for us, too."

"And that is?" Their kiss was long and slow, soft and sweet, as Merri prepared to take that final leap of faith with him.

"Loving each other every day for the rest of our lives."

Epilogue

"His eyes are all squinty." Six-year-old Jessalyn scowled.

"Yeah. And he doesn't have much hair and he's all red and wrinkly," Jeffrey complained.

Merri and Chase were prepared for this. They'd taken the hospital's class on sibling and newborn bonding. "That's because all babies look like this when they are born," Chase told the rising first-graders calmly.

"Want to see the pictures we took of you on your first day in the hospital?" Merri asked.

The pair nodded and climbed closer to her on the bed.

Chase took baby Andrew and handed Merri the little book of photographs they had prepared. The twins studied the portraits carefully. "Which one am I?" Jessalyn asked finally.

Merri pointed her out. "You're the one in pink, because you're a girl."

"And I'm the one in blue because I'm a boy," Jeffrey deduced.

The adults exchanged tender looks.

"That's right," Merri said, wrapping her arms around the two and folding them close. She breathed in their sweet, familiar scents. "And you were both incredibly cute, even with red, wrinkly skin, fuzzy hair and squinty eyes."

They both grinned, pleased. "Can he play with us now?" Jessalyn asked.

"Maybe get in the stroller and go outside?" Jeffrey suggested.

Chase and Merri exchanged amused glances this time. "He's not ready for that yet," Chase told the kids affectionately, "but he can hang out with all of us now, right here."

The twins sighed. Each snuck a look at baby Andrew and smiled again, broadly this time.

"They seemed to take the introduction well," Chase remarked twenty minutes later, when they'd gone off with Paige and Kurt and the triplets for some cafeteria ice cream.

Merri relished her time alone with Chase. She clasped his hand and squeezed it. "I thought so."

"In fact, this whole last year and a half has gone really well." He sat on the bed next to her, facing her. Together, they admired their new baby. Andrew was healthy and strong. He had Chase's nose and her eyes, the twins cherubic lips and stubborn chin.

Love filled Merri's heart. Every one of her dreams had come true. "I know it's July…"

Chase stroked her cheek and gazed deep into her eyes. "But it kind of feels like Christmas, doesn't it?"

Merri nodded emotionally. What had started out as a point of honor had become so much more. She and Chase had found love. The wrongs of the past had been righted, on the home front and in court. The twins had a daddy and a mommy, as well as a new baby brother. And most of all, Merri and Chase knew the utter joy that faith and hope could bring to a family and each other. "We're just so blessed," she whispered, tears of happiness filling her eyes.

His own eyes gleaming, Chase kissed her tenderly. "I couldn't agree with you more."

* * * * *

Watch for the next book in Cathy Gillen Thacker's
LEGENDS OF LARAMIE COUNTY *miniseries—*
THE TEXAS RANCHER'S FAMILY,
coming in February 2013 only from
Harlequin American Romance!

COMING NEXT MONTH
from Harlequin® American Romance®

AVAILABLE NOVEMBER 20, 2012

#1429 TOMAS: COWBOY HOMECOMING
Harts of the Rodeo
Linda Warren
Tomas Hart has finally come home to Montana and his family, but it's single mom Cheyenne Sundell who captures the ex-marine's attention. Too bad she's wary of wounded soldiers—for good reason.

#1430 THE SEAL'S STOLEN CHILD
Operation: Family
Laura Marie Altom
Navy SEAL Garrett Solomon has been to hell and back, but his missions were nothing compared to learning he has fathered a son. Now he and Eve Barnesworth just have to find him....

#1431 RANCHER'S SON
Fatherhood
Leigh Duncan
Bloodlines are everything to cattle rancher Ty Parker, so he's stunned when beautiful social worker Sarah Magarity claims he has a little boy. Is the child really his?

#1432 THE DADDY PROJECT
Lee McKenzie
Nate McTavish is a single dad juggling house, job and twin daughters. He hires Kristi Callahan to help with the house, but she quickly realizes Nate is a much bigger project!

You can find more information on upcoming Harlequin® titles, free excerpts and more at www.Harlequin.com.

REQUEST YOUR FREE BOOKS!
2 FREE NOVELS PLUS 2 FREE GIFTS!

◆ Harlequin®

American ★ Romance®

LOVE, HOME & HAPPINESS

YES! Please send me 2 FREE Harlequin® American Romance® novels and my 2 FREE gifts (gifts are worth about $10). After receiving them, if I don't wish to receive any more books, I can return the shipping statement marked "cancel." If I don't cancel, I will receive 4 brand-new novels every month and be billed just $4.49 per book in the U.S. or $5.24 per book in Canada. That's a saving of at least 14% off the cover price! It's quite a bargain! Shipping and handling is just 50¢ per book in the U.S. and 75¢ per book in Canada.* I understand that accepting the 2 free books and gifts places me under no obligation to buy anything. I can always return a shipment and cancel at any time. Even if I never buy another book, the two free books and gifts are mine to keep forever.

154/354 HDN FEP2

Name _____ (PLEASE PRINT)

Address _____ Apt. #

City _____ State/Prov. _____ Zip/Postal Code

Signature (if under 18, a parent or guardian must sign)

Mail to the **Reader Service:**
IN U.S.A.: P.O. Box 1867, Buffalo, NY 14240-1867
IN CANADA: P.O. Box 609, Fort Erie, Ontario L2A 5X3

Not valid for current subscribers to Harlequin American Romance books.

Want to try two free books from another line?
Call 1-800-873-8635 or visit www.ReaderService.com.

* Terms and prices subject to change without notice. Prices do not include applicable taxes. Sales tax applicable in N.Y. Canadian residents will be charged applicable taxes. Offer not valid in Quebec. This offer is limited to one order per household. All orders subject to credit approval. Credit or debit balances in a customer's account(s) may be offset by any other outstanding balance owed by or to the customer. Please allow 4 to 6 weeks for delivery. Offer available while quantities last.

Your Privacy—The Reader Service is committed to protecting your privacy. Our Privacy Policy is available online at www.ReaderService.com or upon request from the Reader Service.

We make a portion of our mailing list available to reputable third parties that offer products we believe may interest you. If you prefer that we not exchange your name with third parties, or if you wish to clarify or modify your communication preferences, please visit us at www.ReaderService.com/consumerschoice or write to us at Reader Service Preference Service, P.O. Box 9062, Buffalo, NY 14269. Include your complete name and address.

HAR11B

HARLEQUIN

ROMANTIC
SUSPENSE

Get your heart racing this holiday season with double the pulse-pounding action.

Christmas Confidential

Featuring

Holiday Protector by **Marilyn Pappano**

Miri Duncan doesn't care that it's almost Christmas. She's got bigger worries on her mind. But surviving the trip to Georgia from Texas is going to be her biggest challenge. Days in a car with the man who broke her heart and helped send her to prison—private investigator Dean Montgomery.

A Chance Reunion by **Linda Conrad**

When the husband Elana Novak left behind five years ago shows up in her new California home she knows danger is coming her way. To protect the man she is quickly falling for Elana must convince private investigator Gage Chance that she is a different person. But Gage isn't about to let her walk away…even with the bad guys right on their heels.

Available December 2012 wherever books are sold!

www.Harlequin.com

HRS27801

The Bowman siblings have avoided Christmas ever since a family tragedy took the lives of their parents during the holiday years ago. But twins Trace and Taft Bowman have gotten past their grief, courtesy of the new women in their lives. Is it sister Caidy's turn to find love—perhaps with the new veterinarian in town?

Read on for an excerpt from
A COLD CREEK NOEL by USA TODAY
bestselling author RaeAnne Thayne, next in her ongoing series THE COWBOYS OF COLD CREEK

***

"For what it's worth, I think the guys around here are crazy. Even if you did grow up with them."

He might have left things at that, safe and uncomplicated, except his eyes suddenly shifted to her mouth and he didn't miss the flare of heat in her gaze. He swore under his breath, already regretting what he seemed to have no power to resist, and then he reached for her.

As his mouth settled over hers, warm and firm and tasting of cocoa, Caidy couldn't quite believe this was happening.

She was being kissed by the sexy new veterinarian, just a day after thinking him rude and abrasive. For a long moment she was shocked into immobility, then heat began to seep through her frozen stupor. Oh. Oh, yes!

How long had it been since she had enjoyed a kiss and wanted more? She was astounded to realize she couldn't really remember. As his lips played over hers, she shifted her neck slightly for a better angle. Her insides seemed to give a collective shiver. Mmm. This was exactly what two people ought to be doing at 3:00 a.m. on a cold December day.

He made a low sound in his throat that danced down her spine, and she felt the hard strength of his arms slide around her, pulling her closer. In this moment, nothing else seemed to matter but Ben Caldwell and the wondrous sensations fluttering through her.

Still, this was crazy. Some tiny voice of self-preservation seemed to whisper through her. What was she doing? She had no business kissing someone she barely knew and wasn't even sure she liked yet.

Though it took every last ounce of strength, she managed to slide away from all that delicious heat and move a few inches away from him, trying desperately to catch her breath.

The distance she created between them seemed to drag Ben back to his senses. He stared at her, his eyes looking as dazed as she felt. "That was wrong. I don't know what I was thinking. Your dog is a patient and...I shouldn't have..."

She might have been offended by the dismay in his voice if not for the arousal in his eyes. But his hair was a little rumpled and he had the evening shadow of a beard and all she could think was *yum*.

***

Can Caidy and Ben put their collective pasts behind them and find a brilliant future together?

Find out in A COLD CREEK NOEL, coming in December 2012 from Harlequin Special Edition. And coming in 2013, also from Harlequin Special Edition, look for Ridge's story....

HARLEQUIN *Presents*

When legacy commands, these Greek royals must obey!

Discover a page-turning new Harlequin Presents®
duet from *USA TODAY* bestselling author

Maisey Yates

A ROYAL WORLD APART

Desperate to escape an arranged marriage, Princess
Evangelina has tried every trick in her little black book
to dodge her security guards. But where everyone else
has failed, will her new bodyguard bend her to his
will…and steal her heart?

Available November 13, 2012.

AT HIS MAJESTY'S REQUEST

Prince Stavros Drakos rules his country like his
business—with a will of iron! And when duty demands
an heir, this resolute bachelor will turn his sole
focus to the task….

But will he finally have met his match in a world-
renowned matchmaker?

**Coming December 18, 2012,
wherever books are sold.**